By Alyssa B. Sheinmel

SECOND STAR

SECOND
STAR

ALYSSA B. SHEINMEL

SQUARE
FISH

FARRAR STRAUS GIROUX . NEW YORK

SQUARE
FISH

An Imprint of Macmillan
175 Fifth Avenue
New York, NY 10010
macteenbooks.com

Square Fish and the Square Fish logo are trademarks of Macmillan and
are used by Farrar Straus Giroux under license from Macmillan.

Square Fish books may be purchased for business or promotional use. For
information on bulk purchases, please contact the Macmillan Corporate
and Premium Sales Department at (800) 221-7945 x5442 or by
e-mail at specialmarkets@macmillan.com

Library of Congress Cataloging-in-Publication Data
Sheinmel, Alyssa B.
    Second star / Alyssa B. Sheinmel.
        pages cm
    Summary: Seventeen-year-old Wendy Darling sets out to find her missing
surfer brothers and finds herself on a secluded California beach, where she
meets Pete, Belle, Jas, and others, learns to surf, helps some of them steal while
avoiding the others' drug trade, and falls in love.
    ISBN 978-1-250-06298-7 (paperback)
    ISBN 978-0-374-38268-1 (ebook)
    [1. Missing children—Fiction.   2. Surfing—Fiction.   3. Love—Fiction.
4. Runaways—Fiction.   5. Drug abuse—Fiction.   6. Brothers and sisters—
Fiction.   7. Characters in literature—Fiction.   8. California—Fiction.]
    I. Title.

PZ7.S54123Sec 2014
[Fic]—dc23

                                                                    2013041346

Originally published in the United States by Farrar Straus Giroux
First Square Fish Edition: 2015
Book designed by Elizabeth H. Clark
Square Fish logo designed by Filomena Tuosto

10 9 8 7 6 5 4 3 2

LEXILE: 780L

SECOND
STAR

I

I CAN SMELL THE BONFIRE BEFORE I EVEN GET
out of the car. It's dusk, and the sun is low on the water. According to my watch, it's been exactly four hours since I officially graduated high school. But I don't feel any more grown-up now than I did this morning.

I leave my shoes in the car and step onto the beach. "Congratulations," I say to no one in particular, to whichever of my classmates are close enough to hear. I've never heard the same word so many times in one day.

"Wendy!"

Fiona's voice rings above the crowd as she runs toward me. Fiona has always had the loudest voice, the biggest laugh. Even in kindergarten, it got us into trouble sometimes. Her arms fly around my waist and we both go crashing to the ground.

I sit up quickly, crossing my legs beneath me, and Fiona rests her chin on my shoulder. The brush of her strawberry blond hair raises goose bumps on my bare arm. My own dark hair is pulled into a tight ponytail at the nape of my neck.

"Where's Dax?"

Fiona shrugs with the ease of a girl who knows her boyfriend won't stay away long. "Around."

I remember how they looked at graduation this afternoon. I was sitting on the stage, in the section for those graduating with honors, so it was easy to look down on the crowd and pick out Fiona. Dax kept his arm around her shoulder the entire time, even though it was sweltering hot underneath our caps and gowns.

Fiona grabs my hand with a laugh and pulls me to stand. "Your fingers are icy."

From behind us a voice says, "Let me see."

I can feel Dax's touch before I see him. I try not to shiver when he takes both my hands in his, brings them to his mouth, and blows.

"Man," he says, "you are ice-cold, girl."

Yes, I think, *that's me*. The ice princess who lives in the glass house on the hill. The girl who closes her door to write her college essays while her parents are talking to the police in the living room.

"I'm okay." I pull my hands away and fold my arms across my chest. "Really."

"Let's get you close to the fire," he says, ignoring my protests.

"I'm really not cold," I argue as he tries to pull me away, making a path among the kids gathered around the bonfire. Instead of following, I turn to face the water, my back to my friends. A group of boys are paddling out among the waves.

"Surfers," I whisper. I didn't mean to say the word out loud. My brothers started surfing when they were ten years old, the two littlest surfers on the beach. And the two most determined. Now I watch strangers surf, boys who remind me of John and Michael, bobbing up and down between the waves, shouting to each other, pointing to the spaces where the water breaks, paddling out and then drifting back.

"Wendy," Fiona says gently, "you know they're not out there, right?"

I try to ignore the shiver of anger that runs down my spine at her words. *They're out there*, I think, *somewhere*.

"You okay?" Fiona puts her arm around me, and I fight the urge to shrug it off. She is just trying to find the right thing to say; everyone always tries to find the right thing to say. As if there were any words that could make it better.

My brothers disappeared nine months ago, just as the school year was beginning. The police searched for them, but even I could see that it was a halfhearted investigation. They didn't think much of a couple kids running off to the beach for a few days, a few weeks, a few months.

At first, my parents called the station every day, insisting on talking to the detective in charge, trying to explain that their boys were different from all the other teenage runaways. But the police had seen this story play out too many times. They had murder suspects to hunt, thieves to catch. Two sixteen-year-olds on a joyride up the coast was hardly enough to hold their attention.

I still remember the last time I saw Michael and John. They had packed up their favorite surfboards and their wet suits for some early waves, just like they did every morning. There was still sand glinting in their hair from the previous day's surf. They never got it all out, no matter how many times they washed their hair. John had been driving, and I imagined I could hear Michael urging him to hurry as they pulled out of the driveway without a backward glance.

I close my eyes at the memory and take a deep breath. I feel closest to them when I'm near the water.

Dax moves to stand between me and Fiona, putting an arm around my shoulders and taking Fiona's hand. I've tried to figure out how Dax automatically became my friend the minute he started dating Fiona, but I have no idea. Maybe there's some unspoken rule about best friends' boyfriends that I don't know about because I've never had a real boyfriend myself. The heat that radiates from Dax's body makes me uncomfortable.

"I left my phone in the car," I lie. "I'll be right back."

But I don't even bother walking to the parking lot. Once I'm sure Fiona and Dax are no longer watching, I make my way to the water's edge, the waves lapping against my toes, higher and higher as the tide comes in. The sun has set completely now.

In the distance I can just make out the silhouette of a boy on a surfboard. He floats between the waves, patient while he waits to take a ride. It's dark now, and he's the only surfer left on the water. But he doesn't look scared. The air around him is bright, like the stars are following him, his very own spotlight.

He makes it look easy, paddling in between the waves and shifting into a crouch. I inhale sharply when he jumps up to stand. It looks like he's floating over the water. It looks like he's flying.

Without thinking, I take another step, even though the hem of my dress is growing heavy with salt water. I move deeper and deeper, closer and closer. The water rises with a gentle touch, the sea wrapping its cool arms around me. I close my eyes and just listen to the waves: rising and crashing, rising and crashing.

But then there is the sound of someone splashing into the water and the feel of a strong hand encircling my arm.

"Are you okay?"

I blink. The surfer is in the water next to me, his board bobbing a few feet away.

"What were you thinking?" he shouts. He puts an arm around me and starts pulling me to shore, letting go only when we've reached the shallows. Water drips from the ends of his dark hair down his face. Even in the darkness I can see that his skin is covered with freckles.

I shake my head in confusion. I *wasn't* thinking. I didn't even realize how deep I'd gone in. I just wanted to get a closer look. I'm surprised to feel that the tips of my hair, my shoulders, even the underside of my chin, are wet.

"My board could have hit your head," he says, just loudly enough to be heard over the waves. "It's a good thing I saw you."

"I'm sorry," I reply.

"Nothing to be sorry for," he says, shaking his head. "Just be more careful next time." He's so tall that water from his shaking head falls down on me like raindrops.

"Next time," I repeat, but he's already released my arm from his light grasp.

And then he's gone.

2

"WENDY!"

I'm lying on the beach, gazing out at the water, when I hear Dax and Fiona calling my name. I turn around and see them running toward me, kicking up sand with every step.

"What took you so long?" Fiona says, out of breath. "I thought you were just going to get your phone." She reaches for me, then pulls back suddenly. "Why are you soaking wet?"

"I'm fine," I say, brushing some of the sand from my damp skin. "He saved me."

"Who?" Dax says, wrapping his fingers around my upper arm and pulling me to a stand.

"The surfer who got me out of the water."

"Who got you out of the water?" Fiona's voice sounds desperate. "What were you doing *in* the water?"

I turn back to the ocean, even though the boy and his surfboard are long gone. "He left," I say, shrugging.

Without even seeing it, I can sense Fiona shooting a look at Dax over my head.

"Don't do that." I shake my head, irritated. People have been giving me that same worried, nervous expression for months, to my face and behind my back. Teachers, when I turned my papers in, not just on time, but early. Police officers, when I dropped off missing persons fliers in their precincts. Did they think I didn't notice it? That I didn't know what it meant?

"It has nothing to do with John and Michael," I say suddenly, surprised at how harsh my voice sounds. I turn to Dax. "You can let go of me now. I'm not going anywhere."

"I think we should take you home," Dax says, the words coming slowly. "You need to get out of those wet clothes."

"You know, just because you're my best friend's boyfriend doesn't mean you can tell me what to do."

Dax finally releases my arm.

"Wendy," Fiona says gently, resting her dry hand on my wet skin.

I shake my head. "I can take myself home," I say, shrugging off Fiona's soft touch and turning to walk to the parking lot.

"What's gotten into you?" Fiona asks.

I spin to face her. "Who are you to tell me that they aren't out there?" I say, and my voice sounds rough, as though the sand has stuck to my tongue and caught in my throat.

"I didn't mean . . ." Fiona pauses. She looks at Dax, not at me.

"Sure you did," I say, and I wonder where the certainty in my voice is coming from when I add, "But they *are* out there. I know they are."

• • • • •

The last time the police visited our house was three months ago.

"You better sit down," the officers had said to my parents. I wasn't sure whether I was supposed to sit down, too. But I wasn't about to miss a word they said, so I stood by the kitchen counter listening as the officers spoke.

There had been a major swell somewhere up the coast this winter, they said. Surfers had come from all over the world, lured by the promise of record-breaking waves all along northern California, from Pebble Beach to Monterey to Santa Cruz. But conditions had been bad: it was raining, water temperatures were low. Three surfers went missing that day, the police said. Only one body had been found. Spectators recalled that the missing surfers had been young—no more than teenagers—and someone heard that they were from Newport Beach.

One of the officers nodded to the other, who got up wordlessly from our kitchen table and walked out the front door. I was tempted to follow him, but I kept myself planted by the kitchen counter. He didn't even bother closing the door behind him, and when he came back in, he was struggling under the weight of two surfboards. The remains of two surfboards.

"Do these look familiar to you?" he asked.

My mother's only answer was to burst into tears; my father said nothing. The boards were destroyed; it was more like two-thirds of one board and less than half of another. On one, the foot straps were torn in half. The very things that were supposed to keep the surfer's feet tethered to his board had betrayed him.

Since then, my parents have been acting as though they're positive that Michael and John were the two nameless drowned surfers. The police certainly believed it; the search had stopped, and I pictured my brothers' files stamped with the words CASE CLOSED. Our family mourned as surely as if there had been bodies to lay inside caskets, coffins to lower into the ground.

But I was never so sure. I sat at my computer and searched for images from the swell, pictures and videos of surfers in the rain, in the fog, tumbling between the crashing waves. I didn't see my brothers anywhere.

. . . . .

I'm still soaked as I slide open the door of my house. My mother's car will be sandy and mildewed in the morning. At least I don't have to worry that my parents will have waited up for me. They go to bed earlier every night and sleep later each morning.

My dog bumps my hip with her nose when I open the door, sniffing at the salt water on my clothes. "Hey, Nana. Nothing to get worked up about," I whisper. "Just a surfer in the water." I stroke the soft spot between her ears. "And that's as much of an explanation as you'll get from me tonight."

She follows me down the hall behind the dining room to the bedrooms. The glass house has cool tile floors, and Nana licks up the water that drips from my dress.

In my bedroom, I leave my dress on the floor and climb into bed. Nana leaps up beside me. My room isn't dark, not even when I turn out all the lights. It never really gets dark in a house with glass walls, propped on top of a hill, looking out over the city. The city lights keep the house bright; I've never slept in darkness. When we were little, my mother told my brothers and me that the lights from the city were our own night-lights, there to watch over us and keep us safe. The three of us believed in our mother's night-lights the way other kids believed in Santa Claus.

The tips of my hair are still wet. Maybe it's the salt water drying on my skin, but I feel closer to my brothers tonight than I have any other night since they left. I can almost hear the laughter coming from their bedroom across the hall, almost see the surfboards they'd leave propped by the front door every night, just waiting to take the waves in the morning.

I get up and walk to the window, looking down at the city lights I know by heart and the dark horizon of the ocean beyond. I picture the waves crashing on mile after mile of empty shoreline, bonfires burned down to ash, nothing but the moon and the stars left to light up the beach.

There are secret spots only surfers know. Places that the police can't find and where my parents wouldn't have looked. I heard John and Michael whispering once about a hidden cove.

Out loud, I say, "They can't have gone far. They would never leave the ocean."

I take a deep breath like I'm about to dive underwater and get back into bed. My heart is racing as though I've just discovered something. My eyelids grow heavy, but a thought works its way into the space between sleeping and waking: *If I search hard enough, I will find them.*

I expect to dream about John and Michael, but instead I dream about the boy I saw on the water, the boy riding the perfect wave under the stars. Asleep, I can still feel the waves lapping against my body. In the morning, my sheets are heavy with the scent of the sea.

3

I SHOWER EARLY THE NEXT MORNING, DRIED SALT
water dissolving under soap, spinning down the drain. My hair
dries stick-straight down my back, and I take my time getting
dressed. I'm not sure what exactly I should wear for a day of
driving up and down the coast, looking for two missing surfers.
Finally, I pick a bathing suit and a long cover-up.

A text message from Fiona distracts me: *Wanna go to the beach?*

Perfect, I write back enthusiastically.

In the kitchen, my parents stand by the coffeemaker. My father
is half-dressed; my mother is still in pajamas. Have they noticed
that the color has drained from their wardrobes recently? They've
taken to wearing only shades of gray. Even my mom's bathrobe
has faded from its former bright yellow, like she washed it too
many times.

"Morning," I say. I take a bowl of cereal to the table, and
Nana rests her head in my lap.

My parents seem even more exhausted today than they

usually do. Celebrating my graduation and seeing all of my classmates yesterday probably took a lot out of them. They each pour an enormous cup of coffee.

"Good morning, sweetie," Mom says, placing a coffee mug on the table and sitting down beside me. Her eyes are only half-open.

Not like the boy from last night. His eyes were open wide, like maybe he saw more than everyone else did.

"There were surfers at the bonfire last night," I say suddenly.

I jump when my father, still standing by the coffeemaker, slams his hand down on the counter. Nana's head pops up from my lap, and I stroke her ears to assure her that everything's okay.

"They shouldn't allow that," Dad says angrily. "Kids surfing after dark. Don't they know how dangerous it is?"

My mother nods her head in sleepy agreement. "I think I need a little more sleep," she says with a weak smile. When she stands, she leans her palm on my own as though my hand is simply part of the table. The grain of the wood is rough under my skin.

When she's gone, Dad says, "You upset her."

"I'm sorry," I say, shaking my head.

"Don't talk about surfers anymore," he adds, his voice without inflection, bringing his milky coffee to his lips. He used to take it black, but since the boys disappeared he started adding milk and sugar. I don't think he can stomach anything bitter these days.

"I won't," I promise.

• • • • •

"Ready?" Fiona asks excitedly when I pick her up in my mother's SUV. There are still traces of sunscreen on her face.

"Sure," I say. "I thought we might try someplace new."

"Someplace new?" She reaches into her beach bag and pulls out her cherry-flavored lip gloss.

"We've been going to the same beaches since kindergarten," I say, backing out of Fiona's driveway. I hate driving; I could hear the surprise in Fiona's voice when I volunteered to drive this morning. I'm the only girl in our graduating class who didn't beg for a car for her sixteenth birthday.

Fiona tucks the lip gloss away in her bag and retrieves her phone. "I need to tell Dax where to meet us."

"Dax?"

"Yeah, I told him we were going to the beach today."

I try to stifle my sigh, but it comes out anyway, heavy and warm. "Can't we do something just us today?"

"But I already told him."

"Well, Fee, you didn't tell *me*." I tighten my grip on the steering wheel. I'm headed in the direction of a beach that we know, determined to drive right past it.

Fiona fingers her phone in her lap.

"I can tell him not to meet us until the afternoon. That way we can have the whole morning together. Okay?"

I nod, loosening my knuckles, wondering how much ground we can cover by noon.

· · · · ·

A half hour goes by before Fiona speaks up.

"What exactly are we doing?"

I don't answer right away because I'm not entirely sure; we've been driving in a straight line up the Pacific Coast Highway, past the beaches I know and past a few more that I don't. I haven't pulled into a single parking lot. I'm honestly not sure where to begin. I should have brought a notebook or something with me, should keep one list for the beaches I need to search and another for the ones I should drive right past. I need to treat this like any other assignment: do enough research, and I'll find the answers I'm looking for.

"We're looking for a beach," I say, which isn't a lie.

"We've passed, like, twelve beaches, Wendy. What are we looking for?"

I hesitate before answering. I take a deep breath and exhale. "My brothers."

"What?"

"We're looking for my brothers. *I* am." I wave a hand at the beaches outside the window, and when I do, the car swerves from its lane.

"Wendy," Fiona says slowly, "you should pull over."

"Why?" I don't take my eyes off the road.

"I think we need to talk."

"We can talk while I'm driving." Without meaning to, I press harder on the gas pedal.

Fiona's eyes widen and she sits back in her seat, like she believes I'm going to drive right onto the beach, over the sand, and into the ocean.

"Don't look at me like I'm nuts," I say, finally pulling into the nearest parking lot. "How many times do I have to tell you, Fee?"

Fiona releases her seat belt and turns to face me. I keep my hands on the steering wheel. "Wendy, your brothers are gone," she says quietly, almost whispering.

I shake my head and look out at the beach in front of us, past the sunbathers and swimmers, to the spot where the water meets the sky. I never really understood how big the ocean was until the police said that the bodies of the two surfers went unrecovered; I'd always thought that things could be found, even in the ocean. Everything I'd ever lost had turned up if I just looked hard enough: keys, scarves, books. Maybe that's why I believe I can find my brothers. Nothing is ever really lost.

I push my sunglasses up like a headband. "You don't know that."

"Yes, I do."

"I think I know John and Michael a little better than you do."

Even as I say it, I know it's not entirely true. I've always loved my brothers, but, like everyone else, I loved them from the outside, like they were actors in some endlessly fascinating play for which I had front row seats.

"Wendy, you have to accept that they're not coming back."

I shrug. "Maybe you have to accept that they *are* coming back."

"Surfers take risks on those waves every day."

I can practically hear the words that Fiona is avoiding. That surfers wipe out, they fall, they break bones and can't swim to reach the surface. A towline gets caught on a rock at the bottom of the ocean and they can't come up for air. A shark can scent the blood from their scrapes and bruises and come looking for them. A wave can crash over them until they are so discombobulated that they can't remember which way is up.

I know the words Fiona wants to say: *There are any number of ways for surfers to die.*

I shake my head, releasing the steering wheel and resting my hands in my lap. Fiona isn't going to help me. Fiona *can't* help me. This is something I have to do alone.

We sit in silence until I ask, "Where did you tell Dax we'd meet him?"

"Huh?"

"I'll drop you off. Just tell me where. You don't have to do this with me."

"I'm not going to leave you. It's been a rough few days. Graduation must have been tough without your brothers there. Last night . . ." Fiona's voice trails off.

"Where should I drop you?" I say, insistent now.

Fiona mumbles the name of the beach closest to home, the beach we've been going to since we were babies. The place where John and Michael learned to surf, soon complaining the waves were too small. The last beach where they'd be now. I mentally add it to my list of beaches to ignore.

I pull the car out of the lot and head back the way we came.

When we get to the beach and I pull over, Fiona hesitates before getting out of the car. "Wendy," she says gently, "I understand why you're looking for them. But even your parents have accepted that they're gone."

Gone, I think bitterly. The word tastes like vinegar. No one ever says the words they mean: *drowned, dead.* Instead they say things like *gone, missing, lost.*

"We don't know anything for sure," I say.

"It's crazy to think you can find them when the police couldn't."

"No," I say, shaking my head. "What's crazy is that the police stopped looking." I undo my seat belt and lean across the car, reaching for the latch to open Fiona's door for her. "You *don't* understand," I say sadly.

I'm not sure I could explain it to her. It's not like I was so close to my brothers. This sounds awful, but it's not even about how much I miss them, not exactly. The truth is that the house is more peaceful without them, and no one is making fun of my pale skin and my status as perpetual teacher's pet. But it just doesn't feel *right* without them around. The house isn't *supposed* to be that peaceful and I'm *supposed* to be made fun of. Fiona looks at me like she's waiting for some kind of explanation, so finally I say, "You don't have brothers."

I pull away quickly after Fiona steps out of the car, barely giving her the time to shut the door.

4

I PULL INTO THE GAS STATION AND OPEN MY window. It's been hours since I dropped Fiona at the beach and it already feels like I've been up and down the coast a dozen times. I've seen so many surfboards sticking out of trunks and balanced across the tops of cars that I can't even tell them apart anymore. I rest my head on the steering wheel, my face close to the air-conditioning vents, trying to cool off. The floor of my mother's car is already covered in sand. I never realized just how *much* beach there was.

Someone is knocking on the roof. I blink.

"Miss?" The gas station attendant is waiting for me.

"Here." I turn to hand him my credit card and ask for regular. Out of the corner of my eye, I spot a surfboard.

"Miss?" he says again a few minutes later. I take the card back, sign the receipt. I put my hand to the keys, willing myself to put the car in gear and drive away without looking at the board. I don't need to stare at *another* surfboard.

But then my eyes fall on someone's bare back. Messy dark hair and long, colt-like legs under board shorts. A patch of sand has dried onto the small of his back. He's bending down over a bike, filling up its tires with air, just a few feet from where the board leans against a tree. His feet are bare and the ground must be a million degrees, but he hardly seems to notice.

When his tires are full, he grabs his board and hops onto the bike. He turns around for a second, adjusting in his seat, and I gasp.

It's the boy from the bonfire. The boy who brought me to shore.

I pull out after him, heading north on the highway. He expertly balances his board on his right hip while he rides, then turns into one of the lookouts and dismounts. He walks his bike and his board toward the edge of the lookout, where brush grows out of the sandy dirt.

I park and follow him.

At the edge of the lot, the reeds grow as high as my head. Then taller, so that they cover the surfer's head, too. It doesn't look like a path at first, just grass and rocks, sharp under my bare feet. I keep my eyes down, following the stripe that the boy's bicycle tires made in the sand as it slopes downward. The air is thick with the smell of salt water. Seagulls shout in the distance.

The reeds begin to thin out, and the sand beneath my feet becomes sugar-white and flour-soft, and slightly wet, as though it was covered in water not very long ago. I can hear the ocean, but the waves sound different here. Even though I can't yet see the water, somehow I can tell: these waves are perfect.

The path opens up onto a small but pristine triangle of beach, bordered by reeds on one side, rocky, sloping cliffs on another, and then the sparkling water. The sun reflects on the ocean like a million fingerprints.

I look around, searching for the boy with the freckles on his face and the sand on his back.

Shielding my eyes from the glare of the setting sun, I can make out the shadow of the boy paddling out, already beyond the break of the waves.

Suddenly, he sits up and lifts one arm into the air: he's waving. I look behind myself to make sure that it's me he's waving at.

He shouts, "You made it!" as though he'd been waiting for me to arrive. His voice carries over the surf.

He turns back to the ocean and begins to paddle into a wave.

"I made it," I echo, too quietly to be heard.

Behind the boy, moving so fast that I can barely make her out, is a small girl with wild blond hair. In between their rides, the pair sit up on their surfboards, rising and falling gently, until they finally let the waves bring them back to shore. I wait. Just under the cliffs, a handful of boys crouch around a fire burning down to its embers, filling the air with a warm, smoky scent.

"Nice to see you again," the boy says when he pulls his board out of the water. I notice that his eyes are hazel, green in the center with a ring of yellow as bright as sunshine around the edge of his irises.

I smile. "I wasn't sure you'd recognize me."

He grins. "You're kind of hard to forget."

I can feel myself blushing. Of course, I remind myself, it's hard to forget a girl you nearly decapitated with your surfboard.

"Who's this?" the blonde asks, stepping out from behind him.

She doesn't look at me but at the boy, who's at least a foot taller than she is. Her skin is tan and freckled, her teeth bright white. Without meaning to, I fold my arms across my chest, trying to cover up my skin, so pale by comparison.

"Don't know," the boy says, grinning and leaning down to muss the girl's hair. They could be brother and sister, even though they look nothing alike.

"I'm Wendy."

"Wendy," he repeats, wiping his hand on his board shorts then holding it out in front of him. "Pete," he says, his smile inviting me to take his hand.

"Pete." I nod, reaching out and closing my fingers around his. His hand is cool from the ocean, and when we touch, I shiver.

"I'm Belle," the blonde says, interrupting the moment. Abruptly, Pete drops my hand.

I smile at her. "That was some amazing surfing."

Belle shrugs, then turns her back on me, dragging her board toward the water.

"You're amazing, too," I add, turning to Pete. "I've spent a lot of time watching people surf. I watched my brothers for years."

"*Watching* people surf?" Pete echoes, his lips widening into a grin. His freckles make his teeth look even whiter. "Your brothers never made you get on a board?"

I shake my head. Michael and John had been surfing for a year when I asked John if he'd teach me. I'd wanted to share in it, too. But Michael started laughing before John could answer.

"Sorry," Michael had said, in a tone that made it clear he wasn't at all sorry. "You do know that the ocean is full of water, right? Might mess up your pretty hair."

Now, standing on the beach next to Pete, I wonder whether things would have been different if I'd learned to surf. Maybe they wouldn't have run away. Or maybe they would have taken me with them.

"Surfing wasn't something they shared with me," I say finally.

"Don't worry." Pete props his board so that it stands up on the sand and he leans toward me. "I'm an excellent teacher."

I shake my head. I can conduct my research just fine on dry land. "No, thanks," I say. "I'll just hang out here."

"Life isn't about watching from the beach, Wendy." He points to the water, where Belle is paddling toward a wave that is about to open, dropping into its mouth until it looks like the wave will snap shut with her inside it. But she comes out the other side and immediately turns around, paddling back out into the water, not even winded.

"I taught Belle," he says. "Look at her go."

A feeling like jealousy weaves its way tightly around my ribs, tugging me in the direction of the water. Something shifts inside me: I want to be out there on the waves.

"Okay," I say, "I'll try."

5

THE SUN IS HANGING ONLY HALFWAY IN THE SKY; the heat of the day is burning off. Before today, I'd always waded into the water one toe at a time, giggling and squealing at the cold, watching my brothers run out ahead of me. But today, I rushed into the water after Pete. And now, an hour later, I've lost track of how many times I've fallen off his board. Every time, water shoots up my nose and fills my mouth. Salt clings to my eyelashes until my eyes sting.

I haven't even come close to standing up on his board.

"The surest way to get worked is to try to turn back after you've started paddling in," Pete tells me.

"I'm not turning back," I say stubbornly.

"You're not moving forward."

I shake my head and chew on my bottom lip, studying the waves. This really shouldn't be so hard, right? Hundreds of people stand up on waves every day. Thousands. Tens of thousands, maybe. Pete treads water beside me as I pull myself back up onto the board and try again. And wipe out again.

"You're thinking too hard," Pete says. "Or you're not thinking of the right thing."

"I'm thinking about getting onto this board," I spit irritably as I come up for air. "What else should I be thinking about?"

Pete steadies the board between us. "Surfing says a lot about a person, you know?"

I shake my head. I certainly don't know.

Pete floats on his back and doesn't look at me when he says, "I'm guessing you're a straight-A student who doesn't like to cry and could turn worrying into an art form." Pete straightens himself out, face-to-face with me again. "Am I right?" He grins.

I look down into the water, surprised that it's clear enough to see my feet kicking out beneath me. "I have a lot to worry about."

Pete shakes his head. "You can't bring all of that with you here." He taps the board. "Worries weigh you down. You need to be light enough to fly."

Fly, I tell myself, looking at the sky above us, seagulls screaming overhead. Behind us, the ocean stretches out endlessly, so beautiful that it's hard to believe it might have swallowed my brothers whole.

I lift my chin off the surfboard to look at the beach. The sun is reflected on the cliffs in a rainbow of colors, like someone painted them there. The light is dancing like fireflies on the water, which is surprisingly warm, like a tropical current flows right into this cove, just for us. The water is even clearer here than it is down the coast. My brothers would have called these waves glassy and hollow, perfect for a ride.

And then I look at Pete, his face lit up by the setting sun. He looks perfectly at ease, like he was made for this very spot.

"Where are we?" I breathe softly.

"What?" Pete murmurs.

"Doesn't this place have a name?"

He smiles. "Kensington," he says, and he makes the word sound like music.

"Kensington," I repeat, the word heavy in my mouth. I look around us, at the beach with sand so white it seems to exist outside of time. The last of the sunset is reflected on white rocks on the cliffs, the smoke from the fire rising up beneath them. And the ocean, which has always existed outside of time: it was here long before we were, and it will be here long after we're gone. I know one thing for sure: I'm not leaving this place until I've taken a wave.

Pete whispers, "Think of something that makes you happy."

Once more, I pull myself up onto the board so that I'm lying flat on my belly. *Think of something that makes you happy.* I close my eyes and think of Nana. Nana's great big paws on my lap; the soft place between her ears. Nana's giant tongue giving gentle kisses, and her great brown eyes, always waiting for me to come home, her tail wagging every time I walk in the door. Our parents got Nana for all three of us to share, but the dog singled me out almost immediately. Even John and Michael took to calling her "Wendy's dog." When she was a puppy, Nana slid over the tile floor of our house like a mop; she had to learn to walk on the slick surface without slipping. Nana has always belonged to me, the way John and Michael always belonged to each other.

I'm so focused on Nana that, at first, I don't notice that Pete is pulling himself up onto the board behind me. He lies on top of me, his chin settling in the small of my back, sending a pleasant shiver up my spine.

"What are you doing?" I ask, but I don't mind how close he is. I feel warm.

"Trust me," Pete says. "Let me take the lead."

He paddles us out toward the wave. His hands move like fins through the water, and he directs the surfboard to just the right spot, under the lip of a wave just ready to crest.

Pete plants his own feet before pulling me up after him. He presses his body close to mine, so that my feet are in between his own, my back flat against his front, as though together we are one surfer on the board, not two. And together, we ride the wave.

The ocean stretches out beyond us, endless and beautiful. I have never, not in a plane, not in the glass house set up on top of the hill, not driving on mountains to get to beach after beach, felt this close to the sky, this far from earth.

· · · · ·

Pete lets the wave take us all the way back to the beach, the board sliding to a stop over the sand.

"What'd you think?" he asks me.

My back is still to him; I step off the board and curl my toes into the wet sand. I try to imagine what my brothers would say if they could see me now, but I'm almost positive that they'd be speechless.

I turn around and say, "I want another one."

Pete laughs and throws his arms around me, folding me into a bear hug, his wet skin cool against mine, yet still I feel warm. He lifts me and spins me in a circle. I close my eyes, so that I can't even tell which way I'm facing when he puts me down.

When I open my eyes, I see that the ocean is black: the sun has set completely. The fire has dwindled down to smoke. Belle and the other boys are nowhere to be seen. I didn't realize that I'd been here long enough for darkness to fall.

"I should probably get going," I say quickly. "Can I give you a ride home?"

Pete just shakes his head, laughing lightly. "I live here," he says, pointing to the cliff rising above us. "That's home."

I step back. In the darkness, I can make out a series of low buildings on top of the cliff. There are houses lining the cliff, overlooking the water below. "You live here?"

"We all do."

"Who?"

"The boys. And me. And Belle." He points to the house closest to the cliff directly above us. "That one's ours." From here, I can barely make out its edges.

"Who lives in the rest of them?" I ask, and Pete steps away from me, as though I said something wrong.

"Most of them are empty," he says, kicking the sand at his feet. "They were built years ago. You know, luxury homes on the beach."

I nod. In my mind's eye, I see the houses left abandoned, expected to fall apart, with floors still gleamingly clean, the windows still crystal clear. "It's so beautiful here."

"Yeah, but it wasn't safe," he says, gesturing to the cliffs above.

"Those cliffs used to go all the way out to the ocean. This beach was a totally different shape. There were cliffs lined with houses."

I look up at the cliffs; it seems like they've been standing there a thousand years. It seems impossible that they were ever shaped differently.

"What happened? Beach erosion or something?"

Pete shakes his head. "A wave."

"How could a wave get up that high?" The cliffs have to be fifty feet above us. A hundred.

"In the right conditions, waves can get as high as skyscrapers."

I remember what the cops said about the waves this winter; the waves were forty feet high the day those boys they claim were my brothers disappeared.

"So the cliffs just vanished?"

Pete nods. "The waves dragged them out to sea. And the houses right along with them. After that, no one wanted to live in Kensington."

"I can imagine."

Pete laughs as though I've said something terribly funny. I blush.

"I better go," I say.

Pete laughs again, more quietly now. "Wendy," he says, and I like the sound of my name in his mouth. "The tide's in. You're stuck here."

"What?"

"You parked out at the lookout, right?" he says, pointing in the direction from which I came. "When the tide's out, you can go back and forth from there no problem, but once it's in, the path floods."

He makes it sound perfectly reasonable, to be stuck here with him until the ocean shifts. I want to tell him he's crazy, but I can't help remembering that the sand I walked across to get here was heavy with water, as though it had been drenched not too long ago.

"And there's a nasty riptide you don't want to mess with," he adds, as though he knows I'd been wondering if I could wade across it.

"Can't I get to the lookout another way?" I ask, glancing at the houses above us. There must be a way down to the highway from up there.

Pete shakes his head. "Not unless you feel like playing chicken with the cars on the PCH," he says.

I uncross my arms. "How long till the tide goes out again?"

"A few hours."

I bite my lip. Water beads up on my skin, drips from my hair. The temperature is dropping.

"Don't worry," Pete says, putting his hand on my back, exactly where his chin rested when we surfed together. Warmth blossoms over my whole body. "You're safe as long as you stay with me."

6

"COME ON," PETE SAYS. HE PICKS A SWEATSHIRT UP from the sand, pulls it over his head, and hands me my cover-up. "It's already dark," he adds, tugging gently on my arm.

There is a set of wooden stairs, practically a ladder, built into the cliffs, winding its way to the houses above. I follow Pete up, but when we're about halfway, he steps away from the stairs onto the cliff.

"Here," Pete says, pulling me up onto an enormous flat rock that juts out over the side. "Have a seat."

I curl into a ball, feet tucked tight against my thighs. From here, I can see the entire beach. The water reflects the moonlight so that each wave is luminous.

"Cold?" Pete asks, rubbing his hands together.

I shake my head, but my teeth have begun to chatter. Pete sits down next to me, pulling me close. He rests his arm around my shoulder lazily, as though we've been sitting like this for years.

And the truth is, it feels like we have. I lean into the weight of his body, soaking up his warmth.

Pete surprises me by asking, "So who are your brothers anyway?"

Maybe Pete's seen them, I think suddenly. This is exactly the kind of place where they would have come to surf. I can't believe I didn't ask sooner.

"John and Michael Darling. They're twins. They've been missing since September, but I'm going to find them."

I pull my phone from the pocket of my cover-up and bring up a picture of my brothers. I know I should probably call my parents, or at least Fiona, tell them where I am, but I can't help feeling almost relieved when I see that there's no cell reception here.

"Here," I say, holding the phone up hopefully. "That's them."

Pete takes my phone to look at the picture, his fingers grazing mine. The light from the phone casts shadows across the rocks and illuminates Pete's face so that I can see his freckles. I wonder how long it would take to count them all. For a second, I'm certain he's about to tell me that he knows them. But instead, he says, "They look like you."

"What?" I say, surprised. "No, they don't. They never have, except for our eyes. They've always had . . ." I cut myself off, not sure exactly how to put it.

Pete smiles at me, his teeth white in the moonlight. His face is so close to mine that when he speaks I can feel his breath on my lips.

"What have they always had?"

I shrug. "I don't know. That kind of magnetic quality that

some people are just born with. Like famous people, you know, so that you just want to follow them around to see what they'll do next."

"They sound pretty special," he says.

I nod. "You don't recognize them, do you? You've never seen them here?"

Pete hands me back my phone. "I wish I could tell you I knew where they were."

I sigh. "Me, too."

Pete leans in, his forehead touching mine. "You've got kind of a magnetic quality, too, you know."

My cheeks grow hot. "I do?"

Pete just smiles. Every fiber of my body wants to stay close to this boy, but still I pull away, just a little, just enough to put some air between us. Instead of looking at Pete I look up at the sky; the moon is bright and the stars reflect off the ocean like a million tiny lights. When I was little, my brothers and I made wishes on the stars every night. My mother said we should each wish on the first star we saw, but John said that stars were like birthday cakes: you had to wish on your own, and if all three of us chose the same star—the first star—then our wishes wouldn't come true. Since John and Michael shared a birthday cake every year, John said, he and Michael could make their wishes together on the first star we saw, but I had to make my wish on the second star. I smile now, remembering how serious John was about it.

Suddenly, above the roar of the waves, I hear something. A low beat, as though someone in the distance is banging an enormous drum. A rhythm so deep I can feel it vibrating through the rocks below us.

"Do you hear that?" I ask. The music sounds so strange alongside the waves that I almost think I'm imagining it.

"It's Jas. He lives in one of the houses up there," Pete says, gesturing to the cliffs above us.

The music grows louder, a rough kind of harmony against the waves.

"Is he having a party or something?"

"Or something," Pete says, making a face. The anger in his expression looks strange on him, like he's wearing a shirt that just doesn't fit.

"Who is he?" I ask.

"He's a lot of things. Including a drug dealer. Parties are how he gets new recruits."

"Pot? Or—?"

"Dust. Fairy dust."

"I've never heard of it," I say, though it's not that surprising. I've never tried drugs. I've hardly ever had a real drink. "Not that I'm an expert."

"Not something you want to be an expert on, believe me."

I shrug. "I'm a nerd."

"If you're such a nerd, why were you at the beach today instead of at school?"

"It's summer. School's out," I say, looking at him incredulously. I don't think I've ever met someone who doesn't know what season it is. But then I guess he doesn't exactly need to keep track of the days and weeks and months of the year here. "I just graduated actually. I'm starting college in September."

"Oh?"

"Yeah. Stanford." I gesture vaguely to somewhere up the coast, even though Stanford's hours and hours away, and nowhere near the water.

"You must be pretty smart."

I shake my head. "Only about the things you can find in books."

He leans close to me again, and I don't think I could pull away now if I wanted to.

Besides, I don't want to.

I can feel Pete's warm breath on my face, his arm wrapped like a scarf around my neck, blocking out the wind. I can smell the salt water on his skin, or maybe it's the salt water on my skin. We're so close that I can't tell. I've never really noticed the moment right before a kiss, when everything almost freezes. I close my eyes. The surf sounds as though the waves are crashing in slow motion. The wind is a moan rather than a whistle.

Pete's kiss is feather-soft, a breeze from the ocean hitting my lips. The sensation isn't like anything I've ever felt; his touch doesn't even resemble the touch of the boys who've kissed me before. Not that it's such a long list; my prom date last month, a series of double dates with Fiona when we were juniors, a game of spin the bottle in ninth grade.

This is something else entirely. Pete shifts his weight; now we're lying side by side and I don't know how long we've been kissing, but it feels as though we've *always* been kissing. And it feels as though we might go on kissing forever. In fact, I don't remember the end of our kiss at all; the next thing I know, I'm waking up to the sound of Pete's voice saying gently, "The tide's probably on its way out by now."

I blink, not quite sure how long I slept. Pete props his chin up on my shoulder, his fingers resting in the crook of my hip. I shiver as he stands up and reaches down for my hand, pulling me onto my feet. "Come on, I'll walk you to your car."

Pete doesn't let go of my hand once we're back down on the beach. He leads me toward the path I walked to get here. Between the reeds, the water is still higher than it was when I first got here, up over the sand and past my ankles. But Pete manages to walk through it without splashing, and I try to put my feet exactly where he puts his, nesting my small footprints inside his larger ones.

"So," I say to his back, "how long have you lived here anyway?"

I imagine the muscles of his shoulders moving under his shirt as he shrugs. "Awhile."

"And Belle and the boys on the beach—have they always lived with you?"

Pete doesn't turn around when he answers me. "Not always. People come and go sometimes. But a few of us have been here all along."

"Yeah, but who lived here before you? I mean, was the house empty when you got there? I guess you guys are squatters, right?"

I feel a pang of disappointment in my belly when my feet hit the dry, hard surface of the parking lot. Pete finally turns around.

"Wendy," Pete says gently, "people around here don't exactly like answering those kinds of questions."

I shake my head. "I don't understand."

"Belle and the boys and I—we don't exactly trust outsiders who show up asking a lot of questions, you know what I mean?"

I nod, stiffening at the word *outsider*. I should have known better. I have to pay closer attention to these kinds of details if I'm going to find my brothers. These kids must be mostly runaways, and now they live down the road from some kind of criminal. Most of them are minors. None of them are supposed to be here. No one is really *supposed* to be here.

"I'm sorry," I say quickly.

Pete smiles. "Nothing to apologize for. You can ask *me* anything you want. But you know what I mean, right? When you come back—"

"When I come back?"

Pete grins, walking me around to the driver's seat. I turn to face him, my back against the car. He stands so close that I have to arch my neck to look into his face.

Around us, the sky has already begun to lighten. The sun will be up, and Pete and his friends will be back in the water. I blink in the light; it doesn't feel like I've been here long enough for the sun to set and rise again.

I think maybe he's going to kiss me again, but instead he backs away. I feel empty as the cold air off the water rushes to fill all the space that he had taken up.

As he turns to walk away, I call out after him. "Pete!"

He turns to face me. I take a deep breath, remembering the feeling of weightlessness on the water, the rush of the wave overhead. The weight of his body behind me when we stood on the board, beside me when we sat on the cliff.

"Thanks for the flying lesson."

He grins again, his smile already familiar. "Anytime," he answers. "Anytime."

7

MY PHONE BUZZES IN MY POCKET; WHEN I REACH for it, I feel sand in my pocket, too. Three missed calls, all from Fiona. Four new texts, all from Fiona. My parents didn't even notice I was out all night. I drive home without looking at the messages.

Nana is the only one awake when I open the door to the house. I glance at my phone; it's a little after five a.m.

"Hey, girl. You'll never believe what you helped me do." I bend down to kiss the top of her head, my back aching with the effort. In fact, my entire body is sore. I didn't even know I had half the muscles I used yesterday. Despite the pain, I feel stronger today than I did twenty-four hours ago.

As I pour Nana's breakfast into her bowl and some cereal into mine, I realize with surprise that I haven't eaten since lunchtime yesterday. I'm suddenly starving, and finish my cereal in the short walk from the kitchen into my bedroom, where I sit on the bed, pulling the covers back and messing the sheets so it looks like I slept here last night. My parents knew I was spending the day with Fiona yesterday; they'll just assume I came home sometime after they fell asleep.

Nana rests her head on my lap, nosing around in my pockets.

Normally, in the morning, the house smells like the coffee my father sets to brew in the kitchen. But today, my room smells like something else: it smells like Kensington.

It smells like Pete.

· · · · ·

"Where did you disappear to after you left me at the beach? You haven't answered my calls or my texts. You can't just be out of touch like that." Fiona sits on the edge of my bed that afternoon.

"Why not?" I ask, mildly amused by the urgency in her voice. Like we've never gone twenty-four hours without talking or texting. Which, I suppose, we haven't.

"Because," Fiona says, and repeats it firmly. "Because."

Then she shrugs, looking down at my sheets. I'm still wearing the same bathing suit and cover-up, sitting cross-legged in the center of my bed.

"There's sand all over your sheets," Fiona says, then looks at me.

"I told you. I spent yesterday at the beach." I'm tempted to add that I spent the night there, too, but I keep quiet, pressing my lips together, remembering the feel of Pete's mouth on them.

"You should have just come to the beach with Dax and me."

I shake my head. "The beach I ended up at was different," I say, and I can feel myself smiling.

"Where is it?"

I cock my head to the side. I don't really remember. I'm sure that if I get in the car and start driving, I'll find it again. But I haven't the slightest idea how to tell Fiona where Kensington is.

"I'm not sure," I say finally. "But I'll find my way back."

"I'll come," Fiona says. "Just tell me where it is and Dax and I will meet you there, whenever you want. We could go today."

I hesitate. Instead of answering I say, "It's a surfer's paradise. *Paradise*. I even took a wave."

Fiona raises her eyebrows. "You did?"

I nod, prouder than I should be since it was really Pete doing the work. I look down, fingering the sand in my sheets. "I haven't felt that close to my brothers in a long time. Not since they left. It's just the kind of place where they'd go to surf, you know?"

Fiona waits a beat before responding. When she does speak, her words sound rehearsed.

"Wendy, I think it's understandable that you're holding on to hope about your brothers. But I'm not sure it's the best thing. Your parents have come to terms with it; maybe you should, too."

I don't say anything, and eventually she seems to come to some sort of decision. She fumbles in her bag and pulls a business card from one of its pockets. She holds it out to me.

"What's this?"

"It's a therapist. She specializes in grief counseling. I've been hanging on to it for a while now, wondering whether I should give it to you."

Fiona looks so serious that I almost laugh, but I manage to swallow the giggle before it escapes my mouth. Fiona likes to solve problems, whether it's her calculus homework or learning how to drive a stick shift. I've always loved that about her, but I've never been one of her problems before. I don't move to take the card, and Fiona drops her hand onto the bed, the card lying in her palm.

"You think I'm going crazy because I want to find my brothers?"

"Of course not."

"Then what?"

"Dax says that the first stage of grief is denial."

She probably practiced what to say all day yesterday, I realize. She probably made Dax pretend to be me while she rehearsed, like an actress running her lines.

"Dax doesn't even know me. Or my brothers."

"That's not the point, Wendy." Fiona sounds almost pained; her hand has closed over the business card, squeezing it tightly.

"You're going to give yourself a paper cut," I say gently.

Fiona shakes her head and speaks slowly, enunciating every syllable. "Wendy, you need to deal with the reality that your brothers aren't coming back."

I shake my head. "That's not the way I see it."

"You don't get to choose what's real and what's not."

I put my hands in my pockets and make fists. Fine grains of sand stick to the insides of my fingers, dig into my palms, plant themselves underneath my fingernails. *Feels plenty real to me.*

I keep my fists clenched and say, "We don't know that they drowned. We have no idea who those missing surfers were."

"You know those surfers didn't meet any other missing-person profiles," Fiona interrupts, but I continue.

"So until I see proof—absolute proof—I'm going to believe

that John and Michael are still out there, still surfing, still together. And I'm going to try to find them."

"Wendy—" Fiona tries, but I stand.

"I'm really tired," I lie. "I think I'm going to take a nap."

Fiona nods. "Okay. I'll call you later."

I shrug. "Of course. We'll talk later."

Before she leaves, Fiona hugs me, rubbing my back like I'm a little kid who's come to her for comfort over a skinned knee. Then she presses the therapist's business card into my hand. Later, I crush the card into a ball and drop it into the garbage, a fine coating of sand falling along with it.

I'm going back to that beach, and soon. But I'm not going to tell Fiona about it. She doesn't understand.

That night, I dream of Kensington, and in the morning I wake up in sheets that smell like salt water. I miss the shiver from Pete's touch. My lips are warm where his touched them; my palms flush with heat when I think about holding his hand. I can still feel his breath on my face, leftover from our kisses.

I want to see him again. I want it almost as badly as I want to find my brothers.

8

THE CAR SEEMS TO REMEMBER HOW TO GET TO
Kensington. It's dusk when I pull into the lookout. I told my
parents I might be late tonight. I even said that I might sleep
over at Fiona's; they don't know that for days I've been screening
her calls, answering noncommittally to her texts.

I slip my sandals off as I walk into the reeds. The sand is cool
beneath my feet, and just the tiniest bit damp, like it's waiting
for the tide to come in and drench everything.

When I get down to the beach, I look out to the waves for
Pete, but the water is empty. The beach is empty. Where the fire
burned, there's nothing left but a pile of ash. But over the roar of
the surf, shouts and cheers descend from the top of the cliffs. I
spot the wooden stairs and begin to climb. All the way up this
time, until I'm out of breath.

The stairs lead practically into what must be Pete's backyard.
I slide my shoes back on and walk toward an empty infinity

pool overlooking the cliff. A group of boys lounge on the other side, and I gasp when one of them jumps right into the empty pool. Blinking, I realize that he's riding a skateboard. He skates expertly down the curving sides of the pool, around the puddles leftover from last week's rainfall, and out again. The sound of the wheels on the concrete echoes like a plane taking flight.

Suddenly, Belle is standing beside me, graceful as a tightrope walker on the edge of the pool. She gets to me so fast, I can't help thinking that maybe she has been waiting for me.

Belle doesn't say hello, so I don't either. Instead I ask, "Do all of you live here?" I can't count how many kids are milling inside and out of the sliding glass doors.

Belle shrugs. "Some of us," she says. "Others are like you—just passing through."

"But where did they all come from?" I don't say what I'm thinking: *Are their parents looking for them, too?*

Belle shrugs again. "Mostly runaways. Foster kids, like Pete."

"Pete's a foster kid?" I try to picture him as a little boy, shuffled from home to home, but I can only imagine him the way he is now.

"What'd you think?" Belle says, narrowing her eyes. "That he just materialized out of thin air for your entertainment?" She stands so close that I think she might push me right over the cliff.

I shake my head, looking beyond the empty pool to the enormous house where Pete and his friends live. There isn't a single light coming from inside, but even in the darkness I can see that most of the paint has peeled from the wooden sides of the house, which must have been white once. The planks of wood on the porch around the empty pool are splitting; some are missing altogether.

"I just didn't know that he was a foster kid," I say finally.

"Of course you didn't." Belle lifts one foot and balances like a gymnast on a beam.

Trying to ignore her acrobatics, I ask, "Is Pete here?"

"Pete's always around somewhere," she says, cocking her head to the side. "Why are you looking for my boyfriend?"

I can feel my spine curving as I sink into a slouch, like the wind has been knocked out of me. *Boyfriend.* Pete is Belle's *boyfriend.* But he asked me to come back. He stood so close. He kissed me. He wouldn't have kissed me if he had a girlfriend, right?

"I'm sorry," I say, trying to get the words out of my mouth as quickly as possible. I remember the way Pete and Belle stood beside each other on the beach; I thought they moved with the easy intimacy of a brother and a sister, but really it was the easy intimacy of a couple. I can't tell whether the heat rising to my face is anger or shame.

Belle smiles, her teeth almost glowing in the dusky light. "Goodbye, Wendy Darling," she says as she turns to walk away.

I don't remember ever having told her my last name, but maybe I told Pete and he told her. What else did he tell her? Does she know I kissed him? I press my fingers into my lips. She must hate me. She has every right to.

When Belle is gone, I ignore the looks from some of the other kids and rush back down the stairs, sliding my hand over the railing even when the stairs get so steep that it's like running down a slide face-first. I can't believe Pete kissed me with his girlfriend just a few yards away, waiting for him in the house at the top of the cliffs. Was she worried when he didn't come home that night? Did she know he was with me? I wonder if she yelled at him when he walked through the door the next morning; I can't picture it. Belle seems more the strong, silent type than the type who would scream and shout.

I grip the railing to keep from falling then run across the beach and through the reeds. The tide is coming in, flooding the path and soaking my jeans, but this time, I don't let it stop me. I want to get out of here before Pete sees me. I never want to see this place again.

9

THAT NIGHT, I SLEEP RESTLESSLY IN A BED THAT
feels like it's rising and falling with the waves. In my dreams,
I'm sharing a surfboard with Pete, his hand steady on the small
of my back, giving me the balance to stay on my feet. I wake up
scolding my subconscious for thinking about him.

It's early. Nana is fast asleep at the foot of my bed, twitching
her legs, having dreams of her own.

I should try to go back to sleep, but I'm not tired. Actually, it
feels as though my skin is buzzing, like I've just had a dozen
cups of coffee, like I've been struck by an electric shock. I swing
my legs over the side of the bed, stand, and walk into the hallway. Nana's head pops up; she makes a human kind of sound, a
little moan, complaining that I've woken her up so early.

"Shhh," I say to her as she hops off the bed and joins me in
the hall. "It's okay, girl."

My brothers' room is directly across from my own, and I stare
at their closed door for a split second before crossing the hall

and turning the doorknob. I haven't stepped foot inside their room since the day they disappeared.

The room is surprisingly bright; I never realized that their windows face the sunrise. Other teenage boys would have complained that the light woke them too early; other teenage boys would have wanted to sleep late. But they liked to wake up hours before anyone else, always determined to get in a few waves before school. I inhale deeply, expecting to smell some remnant of John and Michael, but the air is clear. I guess time can erase anything.

Nana hovers in the doorway, like even she knows what I'm ignoring, the unspoken rule laid down by my parents: we are not supposed to even look inside this room. It's been left exactly as it was the day the boys left. The police searched it months ago, hunting for some clue to where my brothers went. They didn't find anything.

I step inside. Two twin beds, the same ones they slept in when they were five. They didn't have to share a room, but they preferred it. Two desks and one enormous shared bulletin board littered with pictures of their favorite surfers, of epic waves. I run my hands along their desks, my fingers leaving marks in the dust that's settled over the past months. Open and close their drawers. Finally, my eyes land on the bulletin board, study the collage of photographs scattered across it.

One picture stands out like a beacon: a set of waves, perfectly glassy and hollow. The picture must have been taken from the ocean, behind the break of the waves, because beyond the waves there is a sandy white beach in the shadow of enormous cliffs, with one rickety wooden staircase built into the rocks. I lean in to get a better look. The water is a familiar but unusual blue, the sand as white as sugar.

I pull it down off the bulletin board, careful not to rip it. I flip it over, recognizing Michael's chicken-scratch handwriting on the back: *Perfect waves*, it reads.

There's only one place I know where the water is that shade of blue, the sand that bright white, the waves that perfect. I know that staircase; I ran down it just hours ago. The wood may look rough and weathered, but it feels as smooth as glass. I didn't get a single splinter, even as my hand slid over the steepest parts.

Nana whines softly from her spot in the doorway and I turn, coming face-to-face with my father. He stands frozen in the hall behind the dog. I hold the picture behind my back.

Dad takes several slow, methodical steps toward the open door of his sons' room, like maybe he's frightened to look inside.

"Wendy," he says, exhaling on the word. "What are you doing in there?" He peers through the door.

"Nothing," I say, shaking my head.

My father steps away from the door, walking backward down the hallway. I take one more look around the room, fingering the picture behind my back.

My father doesn't look at me.

"When I saw the door open, for a second I thought . . ."

He doesn't finish his sentence, but I can see the hope disappear from his face, like a wave receding from the sand.

"I'm sorry, Dad. I won't do it again."

He smiles weakly and turns away, heading to the kitchen. In a few minutes, I hear the sound of the percolator and smell coffee drifting through the house.

Back in my room, I put the picture on my desk and stare at it for a few minutes. My brothers were in Kensington. *Of course* my brothers were there. *Of course* Kensington was the hidden cove I heard them talking about. They'd always had a knack for finding the best waves, were always sneaking off to new beaches in search of the next great ride. It drove my parents crazy; we'd wake up on a random weekday morning and the boys would already be gone, driving somewhere down the coast, cutting school to get to some beach we'd never heard of. When they first ran away, we thought maybe that was all they were doing, and once the waves died down, they'd be back home.

Now, I think they must have run to Kensington, at least at first, to live by the beach with the perfect waves. There were so many kids there last night. Someone there *must* have met my brothers. Maybe someone there surfed with them. Maybe someone there knows where they are right now.

· · · · ·

When my brothers were younger, I used to create elaborate scavenger hunts for them, complete with treasure maps and coded clues that they had to decipher. Each clue led to another clue that led to another clue that led to a silly little treasure, like a cookie or, eventually, a cake of wax for their boards. Sometimes these hunts went on for days or weeks. One particularly tricky one that I made for their eleventh birthday lasted a month and ended with their birthday present, a gift certificate to their favorite surf shop.

The photograph on the bulletin board is a clue.

Maybe they left it for me. They must have known I would find it. It's my turn to go on a scavenger hunt, and I have to be a better detective than I have been so far. I missed so many clues already: I didn't see that Pete and Belle were a couple. I kissed him and went back to find him, when I should have been looking for my brothers. Next time, I'll do better. I won't lose my focus again.

And if the squatters and runaways in Kensington don't exactly warm to strangers coming around and asking questions, I'll just have to make sure I don't stay a stranger for long.

I get ready quickly. When I shower, I rinse off a patch of sand that's stuck to the small of my back, just where Pete's hand rested in my dreams. I pack a duffel bag full to overflowing with warm dark clothes for cool nights on the beach, cash I've gotten from relatives as graduation gifts, a notebook, a block of surf wax pilfered from the supply in my brothers' room. I feel like I should pack a magnifying glass, a set of walkie-talkies. The prize at the end of this scavenger hunt will be John and Michael themselves.

Nana follows me to the driveway when I load the duffel bag into the car.

"You can't come with me. Not this time, girl."

My father's voice makes me jump. "Go with you where?"

He's holding a cup of coffee, his bathrobe tied loosely around his waist.

The lie comes to me so easily, it's shocking.

"My road trip," I say. "With Fiona. Remember?" Fiona and I have been talking about taking a road trip after graduation for years, since before we even had our driver's licenses. We got our parents to agree to it when we were in the tenth grade. We were going to drive up the coast, spend some time just the two of us before moving away to our respective colleges. But ever since Fiona began dating Dax, she'd stopped talking about our trip, and I stopped bringing it up. I can't even remember the last time we spent a full day together without him.

But my parents don't know that. "I'll just be gone a couple weeks, remember? Mom said I could take her car."

"Oh," he says. "Of course. Must have slipped my mind."

I shrug. "It's okay, Dad."

"Do you need anything?" He reaches into the pockets of his bathrobe as if he expects to find something in there for me.

I shake my head. "Nope. I've got everything I need." It's the last lie I'll tell him today. "Say goodbye to Mom for me when she gets up," I add, and he nods and walks back to the house. I wait until he's out of sight before dragging two of my brothers' surfboards from the garage and loading them into the car. They're so long that I have to roll down the windows in the backseat so that the ends of the boards can stick out the sides.

Before I get in the car, I crouch down to kiss Nana goodbye. "You keep an eye on them for me, girl. I need you to take care of them this time."

I pull away slowly, watching the glass house recede in my rearview mirror. I turn east instead of north. Before I can head back to Kensington, I have to talk to Fiona.

"PLEASE, FEE," I BEG. "I REALLY THINK I NEED THIS
time."

We're sitting on the terrace behind Fiona's house, which is
held up on stilts driven deep into the earth below us. Her house
perches at the top of a hill, just like mine. But you can't see the
ocean from here. We're surrounded by woods, and the air is
heavy with the scent of eucalyptus trees.

"You were right," I say. "I just need some time by myself. I'm
going to drive up the coast, check into a little hotel on the water,
and . . ." I pause, trying to think of something that Fiona will
approve of. Finally, I say, "Spend some time alone with my
thoughts."

"Well, why didn't you tell your parents that? Why did you
have to say that you and I were going off on a road trip together?"

"Fee, you know what my parents are like. They'd never let
me go off alone, not after John and Michael . . ." I trail off.

"I don't like lying to them," Fiona says, sitting up so straight that I imagine someone's placed an invisible ruler along her spine. I think suddenly of the time in sixth grade when I saw a test on our teacher's desk a few days before we were supposed to take it and told Fiona the questions. She was so excited—a guaranteed A! It wasn't really cheating, she said, since I saw the test by accident and we were still going to have to study the answers to those questions. I played along for a while, but the morning of the test I found myself standing at the teacher's desk, begging to be given different questions. Now, I almost smile at the role reversal.

"I know," I say. "And I can explain everything to them when I get back, I promise. I just can't deal with their worry right now."

Fiona nods knowingly. "I'll do it," she says finally. "If they call me, I'll say you're in the shower or drying your hair or whatever."

I smile and lean forward, placing my hand over hers. "Thank you."

Later, Fiona walks me to my car.

She pulls me into a hug, and I squeeze her tightly, sorry for lying; sorrier still that I can't tell her the truth.

•　•　•　•　•

The scent of eucalyptus is replaced by salt water as I drive from Fiona's neighborhood down toward the ocean. This time, I drive past the lookout parking lot on my left, turning instead up a curving road to the cliffs above, where the houses sit.

The road winds around the rocks, like whoever built it was trying to disturb as little of nature as possible. When I finally reach the top of the cliffs, there's only one house in sight, but it's not Pete's. I step on the brake and let the car idle. I must have made a wrong turn. But how can I have made a wrong turn? There was only one road.

The house in front of me actually looks a lot like Pete's. It's the same house—the same design—except for the fact that it's not quite so run-down. Someone must have repainted it recently; this near the ocean, exposed to the salty air, homes aren't usually so smooth and bright. There's a car in the driveway, a navy blue truck, the bottom half of which is covered in sand. Looking at this house, I'm certain that in its backyard is a pool filled with gleaming blue water. I can almost taste the chlorine.

Suddenly, the garage door begins to open. I pull right into the driveway, along the passenger side of the truck. I just need directions down to the beach from here. I open my door, careful not to hit the side of the truck. It's obvious that the person who owns it takes good care of it.

I can hear some whistling on the other side of the truck, hosing the sand off from the driver's side.

I see his feet first; bare and dark tan. They grip the concrete driveway the way a surfer's feet grip a board.

"Excuse me?"

The guy stops whistling and steps out from behind the truck. He's young and startlingly handsome; his eyes are bright blue, and his dark hair is still wet from this morning's surf. He's wearing only board shorts, damp with spray from the hose.

"You headed for the beach?" he asks.

I nod. "Yeah. I thought I was turning into the lookout, but I ended up here."

"You surf?" he asks, glancing at the boards sticking out of my car. He smiles, his eyes as clear as a Siberian husky's.

I shake my head. I've always thought that you could tell just by looking at me: I'm not a surfer.

"Not really," I answer. "Not like you," I add, gesturing to the collection in his garage. It's big enough to fit at least two cars inside, but instead it's filled to capacity with surfboards. I've never seen so many surfboards in my life: stand-up paddleboards that seem three times my height, shorter boards that look kind of like water skis or snowboards, with salt-stained foot straps and sharp fins that I'll learn later are for tow-in big-wave surfing. There is even one hydrofoil board, something I've only ever seen pictures of in my brothers' magazines, plus a beat-up Jet Ski painted camouflage green. And there are dozens of traditional surfboards, ranging from about six to nine feet.

He breaks his gaze with me long enough to glance behind him at his collection. "Those," he says, shrugging. "Haven't used most of those in a long time."

He bends down, picks up the hose, and turns back to his truck. He uses the hose to point. "You can take the stairs down to the beach if you follow that road."

I look over my shoulder in the direction he's pointing. You'd never know there was a road if someone didn't point it out.

"Not much of a road," I say.

He shrugs. "Yeah. Nowadays no one much drives in that direction, so the reeds kind of took over. You'll make it though," he says, gesturing to my SUV.

"Right," I say, opening my car door. Before I pull away, I roll my window down.

"Thanks," I shout to him.

"What for?"

"For pointing me in the right direction."

He shrugs and smiles easily. "You'll have to let me know whether it turns out to be the right direction or not."

II

THE ROAD LEADS TO PETE'S DRIVEWAY. TECHNI-
cally, it leads to the top of the stairs that go down to the beach,
but the stairs snake up behind Pete's house, so I find myself
parking just outside his driveway. I could have pulled all the way
into the garage; the door is wide open and the room is empty,
the complete opposite of the house I just left behind.

I consider knocking on Pete's door. Maybe he can help me. I
shake my head, get out of my car, and head for the stairs, climbing down to the beach, bringing my notebook with the photo
from my brothers' room with me.

Once on the beach I can see that there's no denying it: the
photo is an exact match. Standing on the beach, in front of
the wooden stairs, I hold up the photo. I compare the stairs in
the picture to the stairs I've just descended. They're identical.
My brothers were here.

"Whatcha looking at?" says a voice I already recognize. I spin
around and see Pete, soaking wet, emerging from the ocean, his

board balanced on top of his head. He grins at me; he seems actually excited to see me. I guess Belle didn't tell him that I stopped by the other night, that I know all about them.

I slip the picture back into the pages of my notebook. "Nothing important," I say carefully.

"Want to head out?" Pete asks, gesturing toward the water. "The waves are amazing today."

I look out at the ocean. The waves do look amazing; *perfect*, just like my brothers said. My heart starts to pound, adrenaline swirls around my belly. I do want to head out there. Badly. But I can't. Not now. Not with Pete. Not after he lied to me. And not when I finally know where to start the search for John and Michael.

"I didn't come back here to see you, Pete."

Pete's grin vanishes.

"I know you lied to me," I add.

Shock creeps up his face like a rash. It's strange to see him looking so rattled, this boy who seems so constantly at ease.

"Wendy, I can explain."

"Explain what? Belle already told me."

"Belle told you?" He sounds genuinely panicked.

"Why did you kiss me the other night when you have a girlfriend?"

Pete's face falls. He hesitates for a split second before he says, "I didn't—"

"Don't try to deny it."

"I'm not."

"You're a *liar*, Pete." I spit the word out like it tastes sour.

"I didn't lie."

"Seriously?" Can he really still be trying to deny it?

"I mean—I'm sorry. I can explain about Belle." He steps closer to me, shadows darkening the planes of his face in the late afternoon sun. He reaches out and takes my hand in his. I try to ignore the electric shock that thrums through my body at his touch. "Please let me explain."

I wrench my hand away. "I don't feel like listening to any apologies right now."

"I'm not sorry," Pete says.

"What?"

"I'm not sorry I did it. Things between Belle and me—they're complicated, but the truth is, we were together for all the wrong reasons."

I press my hands together, trying to rub away the memory of his touch. "*Were* together?"

Pete nods. "Yeah. I broke up with her."

I swallow. "Look, I don't want to be a home wrecker . . ."

Pete smiles, and suddenly I'm furious.

"Is this just some kind of joke to you? Am I a joke?"

"Of course not," Pete says quickly. "It's just funny to think of you as a home wrecker. You probably have a nicer home than any of us."

I don't say anything.

Pete shakes his head. "Look. You're not breaking up anything. Things went wrong with me and Belle a long time ago. But maybe it took meeting you for me to finally face it."

I take a deep breath, trying to ignore the warmth that creeps up from my belly at his words. "It doesn't matter," I say softly. "You're not the reason I came back here."

"Why did you come back here?"

"My brothers."

Pete shakes his head. "Wendy, I told you—"

"I know, I know. You don't know them. But they *were* here."

"How do you know that?"

"I found a picture of Kensington in their room," I say proudly. "*Perfect waves.* They surfed this beach."

"Just because they were here once doesn't mean—"

I cut him off. "Someone here might remember them."

I think he's about to contradict me, but instead he says, "Okay. Let me help you."

I'm surprised by his offer, but despite everything I'm not about to turn it down, either. After all, he's the only person I know in Kensington, and I have to start somewhere. "How can you help?"

"Well, for starters, I can give you a place to stay here in Kensie."

"What, at your house?"

"Were you planning on camping out down here at the beach?"

I shake my head, but the truth is, I haven't planned much of anything at all.

Pete smiles when he realizes I'm considering it. "There's plenty of room," he says, heading in the direction of the stairs. I can't think of a better idea, so I follow him.

"Just one thing, Wendy," Pete says.

"What's that?"

"We'll have to make sure it's cool with everyone."

"What do you mean?"

"You'll see."

On top of the cliffs, I get in my car, and this time I drive right into Pete's driveway. He lifts my duffel bag from the backseat, where it's wedged beneath John's and Michael's surfboards.

In Pete's living room, sitting on a beat-up couch, are three boys I recognize from the bonfire my first night here, their hair soaked from the sea, surfboards strewn on the floor around them. Perched on top of the kitchen counter off to the side of the room is Belle, her board lying flat beside her. It's at least twice as tall as she is.

Pete and I have barely stepped inside the front door when Belle says, "What's she doing here?" The other boys look from Belle to Pete to me, waiting for an explanation.

Before Pete can say a word, I begin speaking.

"I'm Wendy," I say, avoiding the angry look in Belle's steely gray eyes. "I'm— I'm just looking for a place to crash." I haven't forgotten what Pete told me the day we met: his friends won't exactly warm to me if I show up and start peppering them with questions. Maybe if they know me first, if they think I'm here for my own reasons, they'll begin to trust me.

"Why?" Belle says. "You look like you've got a nice plush home to crash in somewhere."

I nod. "I do. My parents' house down the coast. But I just can't take being around them right now. It's been a really rough year at home. My parents—they're in a bad place, and I'm . . ." I pause. "I am, too, I guess. I just needed to come somewhere a little bit . . ." I bite my lip, looking out the window at the setting sun. "To get away, I guess."

I take a deep breath, before I add, "And I want to learn to surf."

The three boys glance at one another, then at Belle. Finally, one of them asks, "Why do you want to learn to surf?"

I smile. "Because I took a wave the other day, and now it's all I can think about. I even dreamed about it."

The boy breaks out in a grin. "I'm Hughie," he says.

"Nice to meet you, Hughie," I answer.

Beside me, Pete speaks up. "Listen, guys, I think we should let her stay."

"Of course you do," Belle mutters.

"It's not like that," Pete says, and much to my surprise, Belle stays quiet. "We all came to Kensie because we needed to get away from something. Or find something."

Across the room, the boys are shrugging as they get up from the couch to welcome me. I look at Pete, smiling.

"Whatever, man," says a boy whose name I'll later learn is Matt. "As long as she doesn't take my room."

"I'll sleep on the floor," I say quickly.

Pete shakes his head. "No need," he says, smiling. "Like I said, we've got plenty of room."

12

I WAKE UP COVERED IN SWEAT AND SHIVERING. IN my dream, it was John and Michael who didn't want me staying in this house, John and Michael surrounded by surfboards as they ordered me to leave. John and Michael insisting that I didn't belong here. Nothing Pete said would convince them to let me stay.

I stand up and look out the window. Pete put me in a small bedroom with a view of the ocean. The bed is just a mattress on the floor, the pillow is a bunch of beach towels stuffed into a case. The ocean is covered in fog, waiting for the sun to burn it off. I pick up my phone to check the time, but my battery is dead. Stupidly, I take my power cord from my bag and plug it into a socket in the wall, but nothing happens. What did I think, that someone around here pays bills to the electric company?

If I were home, Nana would be sleeping on the edge of my bed. She would have heard me wake up and would have curled up next to me, the same way she's done every time I've had a bad dream since I was ten years old.

But here, there is no one to comfort me. In fact, the house seems strangely still, not as though I'm the only one awake at this hour, but as though I'm the only one here at all. The only sound is the roar of the ocean in the distance. I count the waves, wishing that I could tell time by their steady beat. I pull out my notebook to write down every detail of what's happened since I got here to Kensington. The name of every boy in Pete's crew, the look in Belle's eyes when they agreed I could stay, even the number of surfboards I saw in that guy's house on the other side of the cliffs. (Well, the approximate number. I didn't exactly have time to count.) I want to get it all down before I forget. You never know when a useless detail might turn out to be meaningful.

I fill up page after page until my hand starts to hurt. The milky morning light is making me restless, so I stuff my notebook back into my bag, turn the doorknob, and step into the hall. I don't know why I'm bothering to tiptoe. The white tile floors are cold beneath my feet and gleam in the darkness as though they've been freshly polished, but I think the chances of that are about as slim as someone paying the electric bill.

All the bedroom doors are open; I glance into the rooms and see more mattresses piled on floors, more towels used as pillows and blankets, but no sign of Pete or anyone else. I can't help noticing that every other room has multiple mattresses in it—mine is the only room with only one bed. I wonder where Belle sleeps.

I walk down the stairs, my footsteps sounding like slaps against the porcelain. At once, my footsteps are replaced by the sound of a girl's laughter, bright but hoarse, as though she's coming down with a cold.

Or swallowed too much salt water, I correct myself as Belle slides open the glass door leading out to the back porch and steps inside the house. Pete is only a few steps behind her, balancing two surfboards on top of his head. Both of them are dripping wet.

"Hi," I say. "Morning."

Belle turns, fixing her intense eyes on me. I imagine she looks at a wave the same way, once she decides *that's* the one she's going to ride, and begins her paddle out to conquer it. I drop my gaze.

"Morning, Wendy," Pete says cheerfully, either oblivious to or just ignoring his ex-girlfriend's stare. "Sleep well?"

"Sure," I say noncommittally, not wanting to think about my dream. "Actually, I'm pretty hungry," I add, mostly to change the subject.

Belle rolls her eyes, finally breaking her gaze. "You're out of luck there, Newport. There's nothing in the house."

Pete shrugs. "Not to worry," he says. "We're going out to snag supplies."

"The house on Brentway?" Belle says eagerly as a couple more boys come through the sliding door.

Pete ignores her and turns to me. "We'll be back with food later. Think you can make it till then?"

"I'm fine," I say. "I can make it till we go over there."

"You're not coming," Belle says. "Wouldn't want to risk messing up your perfect record, would we?"

Understanding crashes over me like a wave; they're going to rob a house.

"I have cash," I say weakly, thinking of the bills in my duffel bag. "I could buy us some food."

Pete shakes his head. "Save your cash. This house is huge. Believe me, these people can afford to lose whatever we take."

"Isn't it dangerous?"

"Not with the right crew," Pete says, gesturing at the boy—Hughie—brushing sand off of his legs behind him. He adds, "And Belle can pick locks like a cat burglar."

Of course she can, I think.

"I'm going," I say suddenly.

Pete shakes his head. "You don't have to come with us, Wendy. Really. We won't be gone long, and you'll be better off staying here at the house."

I shake my head. "I'm going," I repeat, louder this time.

"It's really not your scene," Pete protests.

"I'm here to find a new scene, remember?" I say firmly.

Pete opens his mouth to try to argue, but I shake my head. I've decided that I'm going no matter what he says, so there's no reason for him to waste his breath.

· · · · ·

At sunset, I'm riding on the handlebars of Hughie's bike; Belle and Pete share a bike beside us, and Matt rides a third on his own. They're smiling; no one seems to find any of this out of the ordinary.

I'm grateful for the roar of the surf, loud enough to drown out the sound of my heartbeat, pounding so hard and so fast that you'd think I was the one pushing the pedals of the bike, past houses with manicured lawns and bright white fences.

At the edge of Brentway, we dismount our bikes. Pete leads the way behind the houses. We creep through backyards with pools and diving boards and swing sets, hiding behind trees and bushes. I wonder what my parents would do if they looked out the windows of the glass house and saw a group of kids tiptoeing past.

When we finally reach the house, Belle's hands work deftly on its lock, and I pretend not to notice just how proud Pete looks when the back door swings open as though the house itself were inviting us in. Belle makes a beeline for the stairs while Pete and Matt head for the kitchen.

"Where's she going?" I ask Pete. "I thought we were just taking food and supplies, that kind of thing."

Pete shrugs. "Belle likes to check out the bedrooms."

I don't ask why. Maybe she likes to go through closets and try on clothes. Maybe she likes to slip between clean sheets on beds with plush mattresses and soft pillows. Maybe she likes to take hot showers, since the water in Pete's house, I discovered earlier, is icy cold.

Pete and Matt move through the house like cats who can see in the dark; I linger in the doorway with Hughie, who's fussing with the panel for the alarm. I recognize it immediately; my parents have the same kind. You have sixty seconds to disarm before it automatically calls the police.

"Hurry!" I whisper urgently.

He shakes his head. "I know this model," he says. "We have plenty of time."

"No," I hiss. "Sixty seconds from the time we get inside."

"Sixty?" Hughie says. "Are you sure?"

I nod.

"I thought it was one-eighty." He turns from the alarm to Pete and Matt in the kitchen. "Shut it down, guys," he says frantically, struggling to keep his voice low.

I shove him aside. My mother used to forget the alarm code all the time. Some days, she'd forget that we had an alarm at all, and when the police showed up twenty minutes after we walked into the house she was always genuinely surprised. After the fifth time, one of them finally showed her how to disarm the alarm altogether, a secret that the manufacturer only shared with cops, he said. The next time my mother forgot the alarm code, I realized that I was pretty good at disarming the thing with my fingernail.

Now I yank the panel off and stick my hand inside. I figure I have twenty seconds left.

"What are you doing, Wendy?" Pete hisses at me from the kitchen. "Guys, come on, let's go!"

"Just wait," I answer. "Hughie, can you shine the flashlight right here for me?"

"I'm going to get Belle," Matt whispers, and I hear his footsteps running up the stairs two at a time. But I don't take my eyes off the panel.

"Hughie, the flashlight, now," I say angrily. My fingernail breaks; I try another finger instead. "Almost got it."

Matt is dragging Belle down the stairs.

"We're getting out of here," Pete says, but I shake my head. Just one more twist and I'll have done it.

"Got it!" I shout triumphantly, forgetting to keep my voice low.

"Got what?" Belle says as Pete shushes me.

"The alarm. It's off," I say, grinning. Only now do I notice that my heart is pounding, my skin covered in a slick of sweat. I explain to them about the kill switch.

"Way to go, Wendy," Hughie says, clapping me on the back. "You sure saved my ass."

I grin. "No problem."

"Big deal," Belle scoffs. "The poor little rich girl probably only knows how because her parents have the same one."

"Well, then thank goodness we've got a rich chick with us tonight," Matt says, laughing.

"All right, guys, keep it down," Pete says. "Let's get this thing done already." He turns back toward the kitchen, and Belle heads back up the stairs. Out of the corner of my eye, I can see rings glittering on her fingers that weren't there when we walked in the door.

Now my heartbeat is steady and strong, my breath deep and smooth. I feel like I'm balancing on a surfboard, having just conquered a monster wave. I follow Hughie up the stairs.

I've never been inside such a big house. On the walls are paintings I'd expect to see in a museum. An enormous crystal chandelier hangs down over the center of the stairs, twinkling in the moonlight. I bet it would be beautiful with the lights on, but we don't exactly want to draw the neighbors' attention.

"How much time do we have?" I whisper to Hughie.

He shrugs. "All the time in the world, thanks to you." He begins skipping up the stairs, his feet bouncing on the thick cream-colored carpet. "Come on!"

At the top of the stairs is a long hallway. I hear Belle laughing in one of the bedrooms. "Jackpot!" she shouts, and I wonder what she's found.

Hughie opens a closed door, revealing a king-size four-poster bed, covered in a plush comforter and the fluffiest pillows I've ever seen. It's the kind of bed you see in a movie about princes and princesses hundreds of years ago. The kind of bed that belongs in a castle.

And suddenly, I want nothing so much as to jump on that gorgeous, perfect bed. I rush past Hughie and leap onto the bed and begin jumping up and down. I kick off my sandals; the comforter is satin underneath my feet, and after a few jumps I slip, tumbling down onto the pillows.

"You okay?" Hughie asks from the doorway.

I pop right back up. The bed smells like expensive perfume. "You gotta try this," I say, and Hughie joins me, bouncing on the bed. I feel about eight years old. I can't remember the last time I had so much fun.

Belle comes in, layers of gorgeous clothing draped over the T-shirt and shorts she wore to ride over here. She looks like a little kid playing dress-up. "What are you guys doing?"

Pete pokes his head in the door in time to see me answer Belle's question. "Working on our balance," I say, spinning in a circle on my next jump. "It'll come in really handy on the waves tomorrow."

For some reason, this sends Hughie into a fit of laughter, and he collapses into a giggling lump on the bed.

"We're getting ready to leave," Belle says finally. She's trying to look like she's above all this silliness, but it's obvious from the way she wears her new clothes that she's enjoying this just as much as we are. I attempt a pirouette off the bed, but I trip and land sloppily at her feet, laughing. I can see that Belle's struggling not to laugh, too.

I glance back at the bed before we leave the room behind; it's a mess. The beautiful comforter is covered in sand; the pillows are tossed haphazardly on the floor.

Ever since I was a little girl, I made my bed every single morning. My parents had to beg and bribe my brothers to make their beds before school, but they never had to remind me to make mine. It feels strange to leave such a mess behind.

I follow Pete, Belle, and Hughie down the stairs and out the front door, where Matt is waiting with our bikes in the darkness. He stuffs our loot into backpacks the boys slip on. To my surprise, Belle climbs onto Matt's handlebars, her new clothes billowing in the wind, and Pete pulls me onto his own.

We speed away silently, riding more slowly than we rode coming here, weighed down by all of our booty. Before we turn the corner off of Brentway, I glance back at the enormous house we just raided. It's so full of beautiful things that I wonder if the owners will even notice what's missing.

As the bicycle moves forward in the cool night air, I forget it all: how awful it feels to miss my brothers, to watch my parents' clothes turn gray, to lie to Fiona; how much it hurt when Belle told me she and Pete were a couple, how my stomach twisted when he carried her board in from the beach for her this morning, when she leaned against him as he rode his bicycle here tonight.

Instead I just close my eyes and let the wind rustle through my hair.

13

TONIGHT, THE WIND OFF THE OCEAN LICKS THE flames of the beach bonfire until I think the blaze will rise all the way up the cliffs and set fire to the houses at the top, starting with Pete's house directly above, then traveling along the reeds to the garage. I almost laugh, thinking about the bonfire we had after graduation, the one for which we had to get special permission from the local parks department.

Hughie and Matt show up with cases of beer; there must have been some cash lying around the house on Brentway, or maybe they swiped a forgotten credit card.

On the other side of the fire, Belle slouches, talking to some boys whose names I don't yet know, a necklace she stole twinkling around her neck in the firelight. I can tell it's not actually a nice piece of jewelry, probably won't be worth much money when they try to pawn it along with everything else they stole. But the necklace looks really pretty on her—it suits her, somehow, even though she's wearing it with an oversized sweatshirt and flip-flops. She's so short that the sweatshirt fits her like a minidress. It's probably Pete's shirt, or at least it probably used to be.

Shivering, I step closer to the fire. From behind me, Matt hands me a beer.

"A toast to the criminal of the hour," he says, clinking his own bottle against mine.

"Ha ha," I say, taking a swig. "Very funny."

"What's funny?" Matt replies. "You saved our asses back there. We owe you big-time now, Newport."

"Well, I'll take my payment in free beer and surf lessons, thank you very much."

Matt grins. He has tan lines around his eyes just like Pete's, from squinting in the sun. I think he must be my age, and I wonder if he ever thinks about the fact that under different circumstances he might have graduated high school this spring.

"Aren't you cold?" I ask. He's wearing board shorts and a T-shirt. I'm wearing jeans and a sweater and am still covered with goose bumps.

"Nah, cold doesn't bother me. I head out there in January in nothing but shorts," he says, gesturing toward the waves. "If you're cold, I can run up and get you a blanket or something," Matt offers, but I shake my head.

I lower myself onto the sand, and he sits down beside me. This could be an opportunity to ask him about John and Michael, but I know I'll have to tread carefully.

"What's it like surfing here in January? The waves are bigger then, huh?"

Matt nods. "Oh yeah, they're really something. Just you wait.

If we get one of those sweet northwest swells coming down the coast, you're in for a treat."

I nod, smiling at the way Matt assumes I'll still be here come January.

"Did you get a nice swell this winter?" I ask.

"Pretty good. It hit the coast up north a lot harder than it hit us here."

I know.

"We still got some pretty wicked waves," Matt continues. "I got hella worked out there."

"Sounds dangerous."

"It can be. But Pete always makes us come in when it's looking too gnarly."

"He does?"

Matt shrugs. "I'm not the best surfer here, you know? Pete knows it. He keeps me out of the worst shit."

"Nice the way he looks out for everybody."

Matt nods.

"Were there a lot of people around here in January? I mean, when those swells pick up, people must show up sometimes, right?"

Matt shrugs. "Well, this place is pretty far off the beaten path. But yeah, we get some people passing through from time to time. Belle calls 'em tourists."

I'm sure she does, I think, *though I'm pretty sure she calls me something a lot less mild.* I can see her through the flames on the other side of the fire, her blond hair waving around her face.

"Where do the tourists usually crash?" I ask. "Something tells me you don't have any hotels in Kensington."

"Some of 'em stay in the empty houses up there," he says,

gesturing toward the cliffs. "Most of 'em camp out down here. Or in the parking lot, waiting out the tide, you know?"

"Right," I answer, nodding.

"Course some of them end up at Jas's house, though they pretty much stay on the other side of the beach. Pete does what he can to keep it that way. Dusters on one side, us on the other."

"Dusters," I echo. I'm about to ask what that means when something clicks, and I remember the drug Pete told me about— fairy dust.

I picture Pete building an enormous fence that slices its way down the beach and into the ocean, Pete's crew on one side and Jas's spaced-out customers on the other.

"And sometimes a few kids end up on our living room floor, but only when Pete likes them."

"Should I consider myself privileged that I didn't end up on the living room floor?"

I laugh and so does Matt. "Yeah, well. We've had some trouble with strangers staying over in the past. You can't blame us for being wary. Sometimes, they're just not the right crowd, you know? We had a few kids staying with us last winter, man—I thought they were cool, but Pete ended up having to throw them out, right?"

"Really?" I ask. I try to imagine Pete throwing anyone out of the house.

"Yeah, they just got caught up on the wrong side of things, you know?"

I nod. I'm getting used to the cadence of Matt's chitchat, the way he ends almost every sentence as a question. But he doesn't seem to mind *my* questions, so I keep going.

"I guess it's inevitable," I agree. "But what about the kids who are just passing through—the tourists? Do you ever get to know them?" Just because Pete never met my brothers doesn't mean that Matt didn't. Maybe he was down here some morning when Pete was sleeping late.

But before Matt can answer, I feel the heat of someone's body sitting down close on my other side.

"What are you two chatting about?" Pete asks, and I swivel around to face him. The goose bumps vanish from my skin.

"Nothing important," Matt answers before I can say anything, standing up and brushing the sand from his shorts. He gives Pete a short little nod and a small grin, ceding his spot beside me.

"He didn't have to get up," I protest.

"He was just being polite," Pete says. His hazel eyes study my face intently, the crinkles of a smile playing at their corners.

I shake my head, trying to avoid his gaze. I don't want Pete to get the wrong idea, even though sitting this close to him reminds me of our night on the cliffs, of the way his arms felt around me. Those are the last things I want to be thinking about right now.

"So," Pete says, "did you have fun tonight?"

"You mean did I have fun robbing the house of a family of innocent strangers?" I say, trying to make my voice sound steady, harsh, disapproving. Trying to mask the fact that I did, in fact, have fun.

"Well," Pete says, "you certainly won the boys over, that's for sure. Hughie over there can't stop singing your praises."

"It wasn't a big deal," I say, but I'm smiling. What a strange thing to be so proud of. "Anyway," I add, "I don't think it helped me earn any extra points with Belle."

"Give her some time," Pete says, shrugging. "Pretty soon she'll love you just as much as the rest of us do."

I laugh. "I think it's a little early to say that anybody loves me," I say.

Pete cocks his head to the side. "All right, maybe," he agrees. "But it's not too early for a pretty serious crush."

"Oh really?" I say, gesturing at the crew around us. "The whole gang has a crush on me?"

"Well," Pete says, pausing as though he's thinking hard. "Maybe not the *whole* gang."

I look at my lap. I don't want Pete to see the smile overtaking my face, no matter how hard I try to will my mouth into a straight line. *You're not here for him*, I remind myself.

But before I have a chance to look up, Pete's lips brush gently across my cheek, warm and soft as morning sunshine through the fog. Without saying anything, he gets up and heads over toward the cooler they filled with beer, even though there's no ice to keep it cold.

I stand up and inch a few steps closer to the fire, reaching my hands out in front of me until they feel hot. Just a few more millimeters and I'd be burning myself, but I don't back away. On the other side of the flames, Belle is doing the same thing. Suddenly, she takes off her necklace and throws it into the center of the fire, sending sparks flying everywhere. Instinctively, I take a few steps hurriedly back, but Belle holds her ground. She's laughing, but I'm not smiling anymore.

14

IT'S STILL DARK WHEN I WAKE UP IN THE MORNING, too early for even Pete and Belle to be on the water yet. I tiptoe down the stairs, shivering in my bikini, walk out the front door, and get one of my brothers' boards from my car.

The board I grab this morning is John's; it's the smaller of the two, dark blue with bright yellow stripes running up the sides. I carry it down to the beach like I think it might break, careful not to let it bang against the wooden railing along the stairs. By the time I reach the water the sun has made its first appearance on the horizon, casting a gentle pink light on the ocean. I breathe in deeply, watching the waves crash against the sand one after another. Each time one wave recedes and another builds, it looks as though the ocean is taking in a deep breath, then blowing it out.

I'm standing at the edge of the water, my toes soaked by the waves, the board propped up beside me, when a deep voice says, "Thought you said you weren't a surfer."

Startled, I turn to see the guy who gave me directions when I got to Kensie.

"You scared me," I say.

"Sorry," he says. "You okay?"

"I just didn't expect anyone else to be awake at this hour," I say, but the truth is, I don't even know how long I've been standing here. The sun has grown higher, its light on the water more yellow than pink now.

"I'm an early riser," he answers. He plants his own board in the sand beside mine; it's nearly twice his height and kind of old-fashioned-looking, the kind of board that's called a gun, I think. He's wearing the same board shorts he wore the first time I saw him, the tiniest stripe of pale skin peeking out from beneath the waistband. I blush beneath his gaze.

"I didn't think anyone else surfed this stretch of the beach," I add, bringing my focus back to the water.

He nods. "I don't, usually. Usually stick to the other side of the beach. It's just . . ." He pauses, a shadow passing over his face. Finally he says, "It's just easier that way."

I turn to face him again, though it feels like I'm seeing him for the first time. Matt said that Jas and his dusters surfed the other side of the beach. How could I have failed to realize until now that this guy is Jas, the drug dealer who lives on the other side of Kensie?

"Well, then why are you here this morning?" I ask, taking a step back. Away from him. The water laps up around my ankles now.

He doesn't answer right away. He looks from me to the ocean and back to me again. I think he might actually be blushing. Finally, he says, "Gotta go where the waves lead, you know?"

I nod, but the truth is, I don't really know.

He smiles and gestures out to the water, to the waves that are building ever higher. "Do you mind?" he asks politely, as though he needs my permission to surf here.

I shake my head quickly. "Go ahead," I answer, stepping away from the water, dragging my board behind me until I'm halfway up the beach, close enough to the stairs that I could run back up to Pete's house if I needed to. I really should just go back up there now; I shouldn't stay here, alone on the beach with someone like him. But I don't feel unsafe, standing down here with Jas. Maybe I should, but I don't.

He lifts his board and heads into the water. Watching him surf is exhilarating; he takes wave after wave, graceful as a dolphin in the water. On smaller waves, he shifts his weight so that his board ascends, floating over the foamy crest.

Like Pete, he's so tall that he has to crouch down to ride beneath the waves' crests. He moves on his board like it's a balance beam, sometimes standing at the front and sometimes at the back. Suddenly, he spins his board around completely, like a ballerina doing a pirouette. I've never seen anyone surf like this, not even Pete. When he finally comes back to the beach, he's grinning at me like a little kid, shaking the water from his hair. He takes a few deep breaths, the sinewy muscles across his chest expanding and contracting.

"You really know what you're doing out there, huh?" I hate myself for stating the obvious, but how am I supposed to know what are the right things to say to a drug dealer / ultimate surfer?

He smiles at me. "Now it's your turn," he says. "Waves are getting gentler now. Perfect for a beginner."

I shake my head. "I'm not ready yet," I say. "I think I need a few more lessons before I'll be able to head out there by myself."

"Then what are you doing down on the beach all alone this morning?"

I bite my lip. I'm not really sure. Maybe I thought that if I just waited here long enough, my brothers would magically appear, conjured by the ocean itself.

"Studying," I say finally. "You know, trying to get acquainted with the waves. Oh my god," I add, blushing hotly, "is that a ridiculous thing to say?"

He shakes his head. "Not at all. All the best surfers watch the ocean before they paddle out. You gotta be strategic, man, especially on big days." His smile is infectious. "Looks like Kensington agrees with you," he says.

"What do you mean?"

He shakes his head. "You just look a little different from when I saw you the other day."

"Different? Different how?"

Instead of answering my question, he says, "I could take you out there, if you want." He gestures to the water. "It'd be a shame to miss out on these waves."

"Really?" He's the best surfer I've ever seen. I wonder what it would be like to be out on the waves with him. "I mean, don't you have more important things to do?"

Suddenly, his gaze shifts; he's looking behind me, and his smile vanishes. I spin around. Pete, Hughie, and Belle are walking down the beach, past the black remains of last night's bonfire.

"I better go," Jas says, but at once Hughie breaks into a run; I have to jump out of the way to avoid getting shoved aside when he lunges for Jas, who steps aside gracefully.

"What are you doing here?" Hughie says, his voice as rough as sandpaper. "You're not supposed to be on this side of the beach."

Jas's voice is preternaturally calm when he answers. "Gotta follow the waves, you know? You and your crew don't own the beach, Hughie."

"Waves are perfectly fine on the other side of the beach," Pete says icily, coming up from behind us and planting his hand firmly on my shoulder. "I could see them from the house this morning." I look from Pete to Jas, confused. What was Jas doing here, on this side of the beach, if not chasing the waves?

"The girl was out here alone this morning," Jas says slowly, carefully. Hughie's hands are balled into fists. He's at least four inches shorter than Jas, but the muscles of his arms are tightened like springs, ready to release at an instant's notice. I don't think I've ever seen anyone look as angry as Hughie looks right now. It's hard to reconcile this Hughie with the boy who clapped me on the back last night.

"Her name is Wendy," Belle says suddenly. She's standing behind me so I can only imagine that her face matches the vitriol in her voice. She says my name like it's a bad word.

Pete tightens his grip on my shoulder.

"Get out of here," Hughie growls. "No one wants you here."

Jas finally takes a few steps backward, out of Hughie's reach. "I was just leaving," he says, glancing at me. He lifts his board over his head and jogs down the beach. We all watch him until he turns around the curve of the cliffs and disappears.

It's Belle who breaks the silence. "Great, so now she's bringing Jas to our side of the beach?"

"It's not her fault," Pete says, his hand still planted firmly on my shoulder. "And why'd you tell him her name?"

She shrugs. "What difference does it make? He knows the rest of our names."

"Why is that?" I ask suddenly. "How come you guys all seem to know one another so well?"

Belle shakes her head. "Screw this," she says, lifting up her board from the sand and running with it into the water. Hughie soon follows.

"Pete?" I prompt.

He finally lifts his hand from my shoulder and pulls me to sit down beside him on the sand.

"It's complicated," he says. The roar of the ocean grows louder as the waves pick up again. Belle drops into a wave expertly, her hair flying behind her in the sunlight like some kind of mystic halo.

"Try me."

Pete nods. "Jas and I were friends once. I brought him to Kensington Beach, a long time ago. We used to surf together, right here."

"What happened?"

Pete shrugs. "What do you think? He started selling dust, and I wanted no part of it. So I kicked him out.

"It's a rough drug, Wendy," he continues. "Once it gets its hooks into you, it's really hard to stop. It's an ugly kind of addiction. I've seen it up close."

"Jas, you mean?"

Pete shakes his head. "Nah, he never really took the stuff himself. The best dealers never use the shit they sell." He looks out at Hughie. "But a few of the boys got mixed up in it. I had to help pull them through when they finally decided to stop."

"Hughie?" I say softly, watching the kid take a wave. It's hard to imagine him addicted to anything but surfing. Right now, he looks like the picture of health. But it would explain the way he lunged at Jas this morning, how desperate he was to get him off the beach and out of his sight.

"And Belle," Pete adds quietly, a heavy sadness in his voice. "And Belle."

He stands up suddenly, and I do, too. I know that I've just learned something important about this boy, about why he lives and surfs here, why he holds his crew so close, why he feels responsible for them.

"Hey," I say, grabbing his hand before he can take his board and head into the water. It's the first time I've been the one to take his hand, not the other way around. I pull him close to me and wrap my arms around him in a tight hug. His bare chest is warm against my cheek, and I close my eyes and listen to his heartbeat; this close, it sounds even louder than the waves.

"You're a good friend," I say.

"I am?" he asks, his voice so earnest it makes my heart ache.

"You are," I answer, and I mean it, despite the lies he's told me. Because I know now that he *tries* to do the right thing, and that counts for something. It counts for a lot.

"Thank you," he says, pressing his lips onto the top of my head. I can feel his breath through my hair, warm and steady.

Smiling, I loosen my hold on him. "Can I ask you something?"

"Anything."

"What were you doing in Newport the night I graduated? Why were you surfing so far from Kensie?"

Pete shrugs. "One thing Jas said this morning was true: you gotta follow the waves. Kensie was a little flat that week. So I had to leave."

"You *had* to?" I say, glancing at the ocean, the perfect waves coming one right after the other. "Why, when you knew the waves would come back here eventually?"

"You can't wait for them to come to you," he says. "You gotta chase them. Otherwise . . ."

"Otherwise what?" I ask. I think about my brothers, of the mornings when they were out chasing waves while the rest of the world was still sleeping.

"Otherwise, who knows what chances you might be missing?"

15

THE WAVES THAT MORNING GROW EVER HIGHER, until they're way too big for me, so I head back up to the house. Alone in my room—strange that I already think of it as mine— I pull out my notebook, ready to write down more about what I've learned about Kensington, but instead I find myself writing in it as though it's a diary, about my frustration at not having found anything, that I can't say the words *John and Michael Darling* out loud, about the way Jas took on the waves this morning, the way Hughie took on Jas. And finally, I write that I can't stop thinking about Pete, about my stomach somersaulting every time he comes near.

I must have dozed off because I almost leap out of my skin when there's a knock on my door. It's Hughie.

"Sorry I scared ya awake," he says.

I shake my head, blushing. "No worries," I say. "What's up?"

"You left this morning without taking a single wave," he says.

I nod. "I know. Those waves seemed a little too advanced for me."

"The waves have calmed down," he says. "Come back down to the beach. Everyone's there."

I hesitate. I desperately want to get back out on the water, long to recapture that feeling of possibility, of hope, of invincibility, that came when I took a wave with Pete. But doing it on my own, in front of everyone, is something else entirely.

Reading my mind, Hughie says, "I'll go out there with you. Everyone else is more or less done. They're just hanging out on the sand."

I smile and nod. "Okay."

· · · · ·

Hughie paddles out beside me, and once we're beyond the break of the waves he sits up on his board, so I do the same. "Let's just watch these babies for a minute," he says. "You gotta get a feel for 'em before you paddle into one."

I nod, remembering what Jas said this morning, that the best surfers in the world watch before they take to the water. I look back at the beach; Matt and a few other boys are lying in the sun. Belle is sitting up, watching us. At least Pete isn't around to see what is sure to be my humiliation. Hughie told me that he took off sometime this morning, headed into town for more supplies.

The roar of the surf is loud but not overwhelming, and I'm suddenly tempted to shout my brothers' names, like they're out there on the water right now and even from miles away up the coast they'll hear me and start paddling back to Kensington, back to me.

"I'm sorry about this morning," Hughie says.

"What?"

"The way I ran at Jas. I'm a little . . . I shouldn't have done that. Not like the guy couldn't take me if he tried."

I smile, remembering the way Jas towered over Hughie this morning. "I don't know," I say. "You seemed pretty pissed. That always adds at least twenty pounds' and six inches' worth of strength, right?"

Hughie laughs. "Right," he agrees.

"What was that all about?" I ask gently. The rhythm of the waves rocks us back and forth, like a mother rocking her baby to sleep.

Hughie doesn't look at me when he answers. "I used to be a duster," he says softly.

I have to concentrate to hear him over the surf.

"I crashed at Jas's place for months, and when I ran out of cash, he put me to work."

"To work?"

Hughie nods, his fingers tapping the surface of the water. "Yeah. I started selling for him, getting other kids hooked on the shit. And for every new client I brought over, I got my own fresh hit."

I don't think I've ever heard anyone sound so ashamed. "How did you get away from him?"

"Pete helped me," he says, gesturing to the beach, to the house on the cliffs. "He saw me surfing one day—not really surfing, just trying to take the smallest baby waves and falling flat on my face. Waves that I used to be able to take in my sleep. The drug zapped all of that out of me. I could barely even paddle anymore."

"And Pete offered to help?"

Hughie nods. "He said I could stay with him and he'd re-teach me to surf. On one condition."

"What was that?"

"That I never touch the stuff again."

"And did you?"

Hughie hesitates, his eyes getting cloudy. "I did once. I thought I could wean myself off of it—avoid the withdrawal that way, you know? I thought, 'I'll take a half a pill one day, a quarter the next. It'll be so easy.' That's what I thought."

"But it wasn't easy?"

Hughie nods. "Course not. Because I had to bring Jas a new client before he'd give me another pill. And it was so much harder to make myself do it, now that I was trying to get off the shit myself, now that I knew just how messed up it had made me. But I did it, and I got my pill. And of course I didn't take only half. I took the whole thing, wanting to drown everything else out—the guilt, the ache, everything. Pete found me down at the beach, dancing like an asshole. He dragged me upstairs and locked me in one of the bedrooms."

Hughie flips over on his board so that he's lying on his back, looking up at the sky. "I don't know how long it took—a few days, a few weeks—but finally that junk was out of my system. For good. I swore I'd never go back."

I smile. "Well, that explains why it shook you up to see Jas on this side of the beach."

Hughie nods, looking out at the water. "Now we just gotta figure out which of these sets has your next wave in it."

"'Next' implies that I've already taken one."

Hughie grins. "Each set has its own personality. Its own rhythm. Waves are funny. The whole world is made up of waves, you know. Not just the ocean."

I nod, remembering something I learned in eleventh-grade physics called wave theory. "I should've paid more attention in physics, but I always hated it."

Hughie shakes his head. "I loved it."

"You took physics?"

"I wasn't always some degenerate living on the beach, you know."

I blush. "I'm sorry. I didn't mean—"

Hughie laughs. "I'm kidding, Wendy. Takes a lot more than that to offend me."

I nod. "So what happened?"

"I had been living with the same foster family for about six months when one of my foster brothers brought me to Kensie, introduced me to Jas." He pauses, looking out at the water. "And the rest, as they say, is history."

"But why didn't you go back? You know, now that you're off dust?"

Hughie shrugs. "This is my home now," he says, gesturing to the beach, the cliffs. "Pete and Belle and the boys are my family, more than any of my old foster families ever were. Still," he adds after a pause, "I kinda wish I'd had a chance to finish high school. I didn't get bad grades, you know? I mean, not straight As like you did, but—"

"I didn't get an A in physics," I interrupt. "Damn near failed. Had to get a tutor just to keep my average up."

"I could've helped you with that."

"If only I'd known you then," I say, laughing. "But if you really want to finish high school, maybe I can help you. Get your GED or something."

"Really?" Hughie says. When he smiles, he looks like a little kid. Not like someone who's been through all the things he's been through.

I nod, smiling.

"There," Hughie says suddenly, pointing. "Right there."

"What?"

"That's your set, Wendy."

I look out at the waves; a set is building just in front of us, the waves growing from little lumps in the water. I shake my head. "I'm not sure—"

"I am," Hughie says, giving my board a shove. "Now paddle."

I lie flat on my board, stretching my arms into the water below. Behind me, I hear Hughie shouting: "Paddle! Paddle! Paddle!"

And so I do. I paddle with all my strength, until my arms feel like they weigh a thousand pounds, until I feel a wave building beneath me, until I feel my board settle in beneath the crest, as though there is some crevice built there just for surfboards to lock into. And I push myself up to stand, feeling my abdominal muscles scream in defiance, willing me to lie back down. I stand up, shaking, salt water dripping down my hair and into my eyes, and throw my arms out wide, trying to balance myself, just the way Pete holds his arms out when he surfs, so that it looks like he's flying.

And then I am. Flying. Except not flying so much as falling. Into the water. Over a tiny little three-foot wave.

And then another tiny little three-foot wave is crashing down on top of me. And then another. Every time I try to swim, to reach for my board, tethered to my ankle by a nylon strap, a wave crashes on top of my head. I try to pull myself to the surface, but the waves keep crashing down over my head until my eyes sting with salt water, blinding me.

Then Hughie is grabbing my arm, pulling me up. I cough, wondering just how much water I swallowed. He drags me to shore, where I have to resist the urge to bend down and kiss the sand, solid and dry beneath my feet.

He slaps me on the back until I stop coughing. "Way to go, Wendy," he says.

I blink the salt water out of my eyes and look up at him, expecting to see a sarcastic expression on his face.

But instead, he's beaming. "Hell of a job."

"Seriously?" I say, my voice coming out as a croak, my throat feeling viciously raw.

Matt comes up from behind us. "Nice wave, Wendy," he says.

Belle is lying down a few feet away from us, her head tilted up to the sun, her eyes deliberately closed. I'm sure she saw me fall, but now she's acting as though she can't hear a word we're saying.

Matt laughs. "Don't worry, your voice will be back to normal in a couple hours," he says, grinning.

"I fell," I say, wondering if somehow they just missed my spectacular splash into the ocean. "I crashed."

"Yeah," Hughie says. "But you stood up first." He smiles, putting his arm around me. "You stood up first," he repeats.

I nod, feeling warm in the sunlight, glancing back out at the ocean behind us. From here, the waves don't look like itty-bitty three-foot waves. They look a whole lot bigger—six feet at least. Hughie tells me that's because before I took off on my wave, I was looking at it from behind—waves are about half as tall from behind as they are when you're facing them head-on. "Your wave," he says, and I feel a flush of warm pride when he calls it mine, "was a good six-footer at least."

"Wow," I say softly, looking from the ocean back to the beach, surprised to see Pete standing at the foot of the stairs, his arms folded across his chest. He smiles at me, lifting his arms above his head as if to say *Victory!* And even though it feels silly after having fallen, I do the same.

My heart is still racing, a million beats per minute. Maybe my brothers felt what I am feeling right now: proud and exhilarated, even after falling down. And I smile, because I've just discovered that the invincible, hopeful feeling I got on the water my first day with Pete wasn't unique to that day—I feel it again now, on land, even though my mouth is bitter with the taste of the ocean, my eyes stinging from the salt water. My jaw is beginning to ache from smiling so wide, and I dig my toes into the sand, hot in the afternoon sunlight beneath my feet. Suddenly, a mystical, magical feeling washes over me: I'm absolutely certain that my brothers felt exactly what I'm feeling—standing in this very same spot.

16

EVERY MORNING I WAKE UP WITH THE SUNRISE. I grab John's board and run down to the water. Sometimes, Pete and the crew beat me out the door, but most mornings, I'm the first one there. Every day I get a little braver, paddling out with no one else in sight, going farther and deeper into the ocean, taking on bigger waves. At night, alone in my room with nothing but the moonlight to illuminate the page, I scribble down every detail of the day in my notebook, but there's nothing that feels like it's going to lead me to my brothers, not yet. Instead, I find myself writing about Hughie's smile and Matt's goofy sense of humor, Belle's dirty looks and the shivers that go down my spine every time Pete is close to me. When I finally pull the covers up around me, I can still feel the sensation of the waves rocking me back and forth, like some kind of lullaby. I've never slept so well in my life.

New muscles sprout up on my arms and legs. My stomach aches as my abdominals develop. But the truth is, it also aches with hunger. Pete and his friends did get food with the cash they made from the raid on the Brentway house, but it's not exactly the most nourishing stuff. Since we don't have electricity, they only buy things that can be eaten without being cooked, things that don't go bad when left unrefrigerated. It's a lot of cold cereal and energy bars.

There's an enormous old grill on the back porch, abandoned by whoever lived here before Pete and the boys. Pete finds me studying it one afternoon, my hair still wet from the morning's surf, my bathing suit still damp.

"Whatcha doing?" he says, coming up from behind me.

"Checking out the grill," I answer. It's not all that different from the one in my parents' backyard. Before my brothers ran away, my father used to grill our dinner every Sunday night. Steak, chicken, hamburgers, hot dogs, corn on the cob—my mouth waters just thinking about it. I stood next to him while he cooked, every Sunday since I was five. He used to call me his sous-chef.

"What for?" Pete asks. I turn to face him. Beads of salt water sparkle across his shoulders in the sunlight.

I shake my head, grinning. "Come on," I say, grabbing his hand. "We're running some errands."

Thirty minutes later, I turn the car into the parking lot of an enormous supermarket. My dad would disapprove. He liked to go to specialty stores and greenmarkets early Sunday morning, pick up the freshest produce, organic meats. But beggars can't be choosers. I wanted a one-stop shop where I could buy everything from meat to cooking supplies to paper plates, plastic knives, and forks.

It's an ugly, depressing building, in a strip mall filled with one box-shaped store after another. Just a few minutes out here, surrounded by cars and streetlights, mothers pushing strollers, businessmen wearing suits and ties, and I already miss Kensington.

"You know," Pete says as I unclick my seat belt and hop down from my car, Michael's surfboard still peeking out from the backseat, "I've never actually run an errand before."

"What do you call it when you and the boys run into town for supplies?"

Pete shrugs, grinning. "We don't call it errands," he says, resting his arm around my shoulder as we walk through the parking lot toward the store.

"You're not wearing shoes," I say as I begin pushing a cart up an aisle. Come to think of it, I've never seen Pete wearing shoes. I'm not even sure he owns a pair. I wonder if this is the kind of store where they'll kick him out for being barefoot. *No shoes, no shirt, no service.* But Pete strides so confidently up and down the aisles that I can't imagine anyone would even notice.

I pick out corn and zucchini, steaks and chicken. An enormous bottle of barbecue sauce. I direct Pete to heave a bag full of charcoal into the cart.

"You sure you know what you're doing here, Wendy?"

Instead of answering, I grin. I know exactly what I'm doing. Even after we've loaded everything I want into the cart, I continue roaming the aisles lazily. Pete puts his arm back around my shoulders and I lean into him, enjoying the sound of the bad music drifting down from the store's speakers, the breeze of artificially cooled air on my bare legs, all the people who barely look at us as we walk past them, people who surely just assume that we're a normal teenage couple loading up our cart for a party, people who have no idea that this will be the first hot meal we've had in ages. I don't ask Pete how long it's been since he, Belle, and the boys have had a real meal. When we finally get in line, Pete stands behind me and I lean against him, my back against his front. Who knew that a trip to the grocery store could feel so romantic?

I pay with a handful of cash I grabbed from my duffel bag before we left Kensie, and Pete holds my hand on the way back to the car. As we pull out of the parking lot, Pete says, "So, Hughie tells me that you're going to help him get his GED."

I nod as I pull onto the freeway, turning on my blinker to change lanes. I've always preferred to stay in the right lane, to be ready to exit at any time. But now I pull into the middle then over to the left, pressing down on the gas.

"He was really excited about it," I say.

"What does he need his GED for?"

I shrug, keeping my eyes on the road. "You never know."

"You don't need a high school diploma to live the way we do. It's not like college."

"Of course not," I say. "But if it's something he wants, why shouldn't he have it?"

Pete doesn't answer, and I glance over at him. The answer is written all over his face: with a high school diploma, Hughie might get a real job and leave Kensington behind.

"Hey," I say, taking one hand off the wheel and placing it on Pete's arm. "He doesn't want to leave, you know. He says you're his family."

Pete nods. "We are a family," he says, taking my hand in his. "You're a part of our family now, too."

I nod, pulling my hand away and placing it back on the wheel. I've never been a part of something the way I'm a part of this.

After Pete and I haul the groceries into the house on the cliffs, I pour the charcoal into the belly of the grill and use my dad's method for stacking and lighting the briquettes. While the fire heats up I prep the food. Pete watches me, and I narrate every step, for once teaching him something instead of the other way around.

Soon, everyone is watching me turn the corn, brush the meat with barbecue sauce. You'd think they'd never seen anyone cook before, and maybe some of them haven't, or at least not for a long time.

When Matt and I finally carry the food back into the house, I'm surprised to see that Pete has spread a blanket on the floor and set out paper plates and plastic utensils. He's even folded napkins beside each place. I look at him and grin, taking my seat at one end of the blanket, and he sits down opposite me at the other end.

As everyone digs in, I watch Pete. He eats carefully, almost delicately, savoring every bite. My own food gets cold as I watch Pete and the boys eat, but I don't mind. It's too much fun to see them. Even Belle is digging in with enthusiasm, barbecue sauce making a ring around her lips—though unlike everyone else, she doesn't tell me how good it tastes, doesn't thank me for cooking.

Pete's right—we *are* a family, and for just a few minutes, it feels like Pete and I are about twenty years older than we actually are, like we're the parents and these are our kids sitting around the blanket. This is our house, and these boys—and Belle— they're our family. And tonight, I feel like I've done a pretty good job of taking care of them.

17

IT'S DARK WHEN PETE LEADS ME OUT THROUGH the back door and toward the stairs to the beach; halfway down and to the left, onto the rocks. The sun has long since set, but the moon is bright and the stars reflect brightly off the ocean. I know exactly where Pete is leading me, to the same crevice on the cliffs where we spent our first night together. I tiptoe over the rocks carefully, pebbles and sand getting caught inside my sandals.

Pete stops abruptly and settles onto the flat rock, which looks for all the world like someone built it there just for his use.

"Come here," he says, reaching his hand out to pull me onto the rock beside him. His hand is cool and dry, and mine fits perfectly inside of it, like we were made to hold hands. Fiona once told me that when she and Dax started dating, it took them a while to get used to walking hand in hand, took them a while to get their steps in sync, to fit their hands easily.

"That was great tonight," Pete says, his smile lighting up the darkness.

I shrug. "It was just dinner. No big deal."

Pete shakes his head. "Why are you always selling yourself short?"

I open my mouth to argue, but no words come out. Because the truth is, it *was* a big deal, and I know it. It made me miss my brothers, reminded me of the family dinners we used to have before they ran away.

"Wendy," Pete says softly, "it's amazing the way you know how to do things, how to take care of yourself."

"What are you talking about? You've been taking care of yourself for—" I stop talking midsentence. I don't actually know how long Pete has been taking care of himself. "You take care of yourself, and Belle, and the boys."

"Yeah, but it's different. You really *know* how to take care of yourself. I just figure it out as I go along."

To me, that sounds like a much greater achievement, but I don't argue.

"And you're such a good person, too. I mean, you worked your whole life to go to college, and now here you are, putting it all on hold to find your brothers. Coming to live in a strange place with a bunch of lowlifes like us."

"You're not lowlifes," I say quickly.

Pete nods. "Maybe not. Maybe now that you're here—"

"Me?"

"I can't explain it. You bring—I don't know—a different energy to this place. Kensie feels different with you here."

"Different how?"

Pete shakes his head, and he doesn't look at me when he says, "Different better." We're silent for a beat, and then he adds, "I don't know, Wendy, I just really like having you around."

"I like being around," I say, the words thick in my throat. "Around you, I mean."

I feel like I've known Pete my whole life, and yet I feel like nothing that's happened in the past several days and weeks even resembles what my life has been up to now.

Pete smiles. "You're getting pretty good out there," he says, gesturing to the water.

"I fall a lot more than I stand," I say automatically. I still spend most days tumbling off my board instead of balancing on top of it. But I keep going. Usually, by the end of the day, when the sun starts to fall from the sky, I manage to stand and take at least one wave all the way back to the beach. I don't think I've ever been so proud of anything; not getting into Stanford, not my SAT scores, not even when I finally trained Nana to sit and stay.

Pete shakes his head. "There you go," he says, sliding closer to me, as graceful and quick on solid ground as he is on water. "Selling yourself short again."

I can feel his breath on my bare shoulder and I shiver with longing, forcing myself not to lean into him, even though the pull to be closer to him feels impossible to resist, a force beyond me, like gravity. *No*, I tell myself firmly.

"I'm so sorry, Wendy," he says, and it's not the same kind of *sorry* that I've been hearing for so many months. First, they were sorry that my brothers ran away, then they were sorry that they'd died. *I'm sorry for your loss*, that's what they would say, and I would think it was such an odd turn of phrase. As though my brothers had just been misplaced and I didn't know where to find them. Now, I think that it's a lot closer to the truth than any of those well-wishers could have imagined.

But Pete's *I'm sorry* sounds different. It's weighted with something deep and heavy; I remember the way he told me I had to be light on the surfboard, the way I had to leave my troubles behind on the beach before I took to the water. If Pete tried to take a wave now, hard as it is to imagine, I can't help thinking that he'd fall, head over feet, tumbling into the waves.

"What for?" I ask.

He pauses before he answers, like he's trying to figure out exactly what he means. Finally, he says, "I shouldn't have kissed you that night." He leans so close that I can feel the heat from his skin against mine. "Belle and I . . ." He shakes his head again, looking down, so that his curls fall across his forehead and brush my shoulder. "I love that girl. I really do. I couldn't stand the thought of anyone hurting her. Even if that someone was me. *Especially* if it was me."

I nod as though I understand, but I'm more confused than ever. He's telling me that he loves her while sitting so close to me?

"But I'm not—I haven't been—maybe I never was—you know what I mean?"

"No," I say honestly, "I really don't."

"I don't love her like *that*. I don't feel *that* way about her. You know, the way I feel about—about you."

I exhale a breath I didn't know I'd been holding, and Pete's lips are hovering above mine before my chest has had a chance to empty.

His arms snake around my waist and pull me close. I let myself lie down beside him, and the rock feels as warm and soft as a plush bed with satin sheets. The sound of the ocean is drowned out by the sound of Pete's breath, the warmth of his touch, the heat of his skin.

He pauses as his mouth comes close to mine, almost as though he's asking my permission. I move my head just the slightest bit, an infinitesimal nod.

And then he kisses me.

• • • • •

Music from one of Jas's parties drifts down from his house above us. A low beat, as though someone in the distance is banging an enormous drum. A rhythm so deep, I can feel it vibrating through the rocks below us. Together, Pete and I watch the waves in the moonlight as we wait for sleep, the beat of the bass humming through the rocks so that it looks like the water is dancing.

"Do you ever get scared out there, on the water?"

Pete shakes his head. "Nah."

"But what about—"

"Waves that hold you down? Rocks that cut you open? Sharks that'll eat you alive?"

"Yeah," I say, closing my eyes and trying not to think about the beat-up surfboards the police left on our dining room table months ago.

Pete shrugs. "It's hard to explain. It's not like I don't know about those things, not like I don't think about them, but—I don't know. They just can't keep me out of the ocean. I respect the waves, the rocks, the sharks. Did you know sharks have been on this planet longer than trees?"

The fact sounds impossible. "Really?"

"Yeah. And the ocean, the rocks—they're even older."

"Doesn't that make you feel small? Surrounded by all those ancient dangers?"

Pete shakes his head. "No," he says, "it makes me feel . . ." He pauses, as if searching for the words. "Some of us have only ever found home when we're on the water. Some of us are always waiting to take the next wave."

I roll over so that Pete curls around my back, places his arm beneath my neck. I don't think I've ever felt so comfortable. I close my eyes and let the surf fill my ears like a lullaby. My eyes are still closed when Pete's lips find mine once more.

Later, when Pete leads the way back up to the house on the cliffs, I look up at the sky and make a wish on the second star I see.

18

PETE SLIDES THE BACK DOOR OPEN WITHOUT dropping my hand. As we step inside, he pulls me close for another kiss, and he doesn't let go as he backs us toward the stairs. My torso is flat against his; I stand up on my tiptoes to press my mouth against his. I don't think I've ever stood this close to another person before.

Suddenly, Belle's voice fills the room. "You kids sure stayed out late." She's sitting on the couch in the center of the room, her eyes glassy in the moonlight.

I nearly fall down, but Pete holds me steady. I'm completely still when I see something on her lap—and realize it's my notebook.

"What are you doing with that?" I ask, peeling myself away from Pete to grab the book from her. But Belle bounces up from the couch and dances out of my reach.

"Oh, boys!" she shouts, her voice echoing off the empty walls and bare floors. "I need to tell you something."

"Belle, what are you doing?" Pete says softly, but Belle ignores him and keeps shouting for the boys to come downstairs.

Hughie, Matt, and the rest of Pete's crew pad sleepily down the stairs.

"What gives, Belle?" Hughie says. "I was dead asleep."

"I thought you'd want to know what your girl Wendy is really doing here."

"Belle," Pete says sharply. His hazel eyes flash green with anger. I look from Pete to Belle desperately.

"Belle, please don't," I plead, hating my voice for sounding so weak.

Belle holds my notebook above her head like it's some kind of trophy. "She wasn't here because she had problems back home and was trying to learn to surf. She's looking for her brothers. They ran away months ago."

I shake my head desperately, a lump rising in my throat.

"She's been taking notes on all of us," Belle says, opening the notebook to the page where I listed each of their names and guessed their ages. She begins reading the list aloud, spitting out one name after the other.

Hughie looks at me. "Is it true?"

Slowly, my head feeling like it weighs a thousand pounds, I nod. "I did come here to find my brothers. John and Michael Darling."

The look on Hughie's face drops in an instant; I recognize it immediately. It's the way that he looked at Jas when he saw him on the beach that morning; like he was looking at an enemy.

"Sadly, Wendy," Belle continues, tossing my notebook to the ground, "the joke's on you. John and Michael left months ago."

My heart stops. "You knew them?"

Belle shrugs, as though it's no big deal. "Of course I did. We all did. Pete kicked them out once they started using, though. So there's no reason for you to hang around Kensie anymore, Wendy Darling. You can go back home to Newport, to your soft fluffy bed with your soft fluffy pillows and resume your soft fluffy life."

I shake my head, struggling to understand. My brothers were dusters? Was it my brothers Matt was talking about the other night, the two kids Pete kicked out in January, the boys who refused to give it up?

Even as I'm berating myself for missing the clues, I know why I didn't see it. My brothers were athletes, surfers. I would never have guessed they'd be interested in drugs. They needed to be strong enough to take the next wave at all times. What were they thinking, putting something like that into their bodies?

My mind swims with the words I'll yell at them when I find them: *crazy, foolish, stupid, careless.* I think about our poor parents, back at home, mourning my brothers as surely as if they're dead. What will they say when they learn that their sons ran away not just to surf, but to get high? It was somehow easier when I believed they left us behind to search for the next big wave, to live somewhere no one would yell at them to put their boards down and head to school, study for their finals, sit still at their sister's high school graduation. But leaving us for drugs? I don't think I've ever been so angry at them. Not when I was nine years old and they decided to give me a haircut while I slept. Not when I was fifteen and they crashed my computer, destroying the history paper I'd been working on for months, the one that was due the very next day. Not even when they refused to teach me how to surf.

But suddenly, my anger shifts, directing itself at someone else.

"Pete?" I turn slowly. I can still feel the warmth of his touch on my skin.

"I didn't lie," he says, sinking onto the couch. Even though we're still surrounded by Belle and the boys, it feels as though we're the only two people in the room. "Not exactly."

"Not *exactly*? Just like you didn't *exactly* lie about having a girlfriend? Just like you didn't *exactly* lie about what you steal?"

"I said that I couldn't tell you where they were. And that's the truth. They left months ago, and I haven't seen or heard from them since, I swear."

Even though it's cool in here, my skin is coated with a hot slick of sweat. I didn't know I was even capable of being this angry.

"I almost told you, tonight, on the cliffs—"

"You almost told me but then you figured there was less of a chance I'd let you stick your tongue down my throat once I found out that you'd lied to me about my brothers, so why take that chance, right?"

Belle and the boys snicker at that, but I ignore them. Suddenly, all the places on my body that Pete touched just a few minutes ago feel filthy. My mouth tastes sour.

"I told you that you were a good person. A good friend," I say bitterly. "You're not."

I stomp up the stairs to grab my bag, digging inside for my

car keys. Before I walk out the front door, I grab my notebook off the floor, where Belle dropped it after it was no longer of use to her.

I pause, looking desperately at Belle and the boys. "None of you know where they were headed when they left?" I ask. "If they said anything to any of you, please, please tell me. I'm sorry I lied to you, but all I want is to bring my brothers home." I may be angry at John and Michael, but I still want to bring them home. I'll never stop wanting to bring them home. No matter what they did or why they left. "They have a family who loves them," I beg. *"Please."*

Hughie won't even look at me. Matt just shakes his head and starts toward the stairs. I stare at Belle. The daggers in her eyes are no match for the daggers in mine.

"They were headed to Witch Tree," she says finally, dropping her gaze.

"What's Witch Tree?"

When she looks up at me, she doesn't look angry anymore. If I didn't know better, I'd think she looked sorry for me.

"It's a wave up the coast," she says softly. I think she's about to say something more, but instead she turns on her heel and runs up the stairs, her long blond hair covering her face.

I resist the urge to call out a thank-you before I hear her slamming her bedroom door. After all, she's the only one who actually said a single thing that might help.

"Wendy!" Pete shouts, following me as I leave the house and open my car door. "Please just wait. Give me some time to explain."

"What explanation could you possibly have, Pete?"

I throw my bag into the passenger seat and climb into my car. Michael's surfboard is still inside; I hate that I'm leaving John's board behind, but I'm not about to go back into that house.

"I panicked, Wendy," Pete says. "I just wanted you to stay. And I thought if you knew the truth, that I'd kicked them out, that I was the reason they weren't here—I thought you'd hate me."

"So that's why you lied to me, Pete? Because you wanted me to *like* you?" I fiddle with my keys, squeezing them so tight that it hurts. "I think that might be the most pathetic thing I've ever heard."

I shake my head, finally putting the pieces together. "That day on the beach, the day I came back here to look for my brothers. I called you a liar, and you freaked out. You thought I'd figured out that you were lying to me about my brothers, didn't you? Not about Belle."

Pete's silence answers my question. The skin on his neck looks bright red, as though he's breaking out into a rash, allergic to his own lies.

My hands are shaking so hard that it takes me three tries to fit the keys into the ignition.

"You were right about them, Wendy," Pete says. "They were special. From the instant they showed up on the beach—"

"Don't you dare talk to me about them," I say, pressing my foot on the gas. I spin my car around the huge circular driveway. Out the window I shout, "Don't you dare talk to me about anything ever again."

I pull away, careful not to look in my rearview mirror. I don't want to see the look on Pete's face. And I don't want him to see the look on my own. I don't want him to see that I'm crying, not just because he's a liar but because even now, angry as I am, there's still a part of me—a part that I hate, a part that I don't understand—that wants to stop the car, jump out, and run back into his arms.

19

I BLINK AWAY TEARS AS I DRIVE DOWN THE
reed-covered road that will lead me out of Kensington. The plants
fold under my car as though I didn't just crush them a few hours
ago when I was driving in the other direction.

I should have known from the instant Belle told me they
were a couple that Pete was not to be trusted. I should have
been able to see through his lies. I'm a straight-A student, a
good daughter; I've never cut a single class, not even on senior
cut day. I've never lost track of a goal before in my life. I wanted
to pass my driver's test, I did. I wanted to be the editor of the
school yearbook, I was. I wanted to get into Stanford, I did. I
wanted to find my brothers—and I failed.

What kind of name for a wave is Witch Tree? Who knew
that waves even *had* names? In my mind's eye, I see a bare white
tree rising from the crest of a wave, its branches grabbing at surfers like greedy hands, pulling them under. Wherever the hell
Witch Tree is, it's where I should be headed now, too.

But just as the road turns from dirt to concrete, I slam on the brakes. Jas's house is right in front of me; this close, the music is so loud, I can barely hear myself think. My brothers lived with Pete, but they were dusters. Are they still surfing, or has the drug taken over their lives completely? I try to picture them skinny, the muscles they built up after years of surfing atrophied to nothing, their skin pale from spending all their time indoors.

There's only one place in Kensington where you can get dust.

Only one person who can answer my questions.

Instead of making the right turn that will lead me out of Kensington, I shift my foot from the brake to the gas and pull straight into Jas's driveway, almost hitting one of the cars that's already there.

. . . . .

"And just where do you think you're going, little lady?"

I raise my eyebrows at the punkish kid standing at Jas's door. "Don't you think you're a little young to be using terms like 'little lady'?" I ask, emboldened by my anger.

He smiles slowly, like he has all the time in the world. "Age ain't nothing but a number, sister," he says, and I bristle at the word *sister*.

"I need to talk to Jas," I say finally. "I only need a few minutes," I add when he begins to shake his head.

"You can take all the time you need," he says, and I reach for the doorknob, but he blocks my way. "You just have to pay the fee first."

"Listen," I say, "I just need to talk to Jas. I'm not here to party."

"Everyone's here to party," the kid answers, and like a magician he pulls a tiny white pill from thin air and holds it in his palm right beneath my chin. "Either you party or you don't get inside."

"What is that?" I say, even though I know the answer.

"If you don't know what it is, little girl, then you're at the wrong place."

"No," I say shaking my head. "I need to see Jas."

"Well then, you know what you need to do," he says, grinning. I look down at the ground, noticing that his feet are bare. I wonder if he was a surfer before he fell into Jas's world; wonder if his feet are rough with calluses from running barefoot over hot sand.

I eye the pill in his hand. It doesn't look like much of anything at all. It could be anything—ibuprofen, a decongestant. There's nothing to it that makes it look any more dangerous than anything in the medicine cabinets back at home.

It's just one little pill, just for one night. I've never heard of a drug that you can get addicted to off of just one hit. Not that I've ever heard much about drugs at all. Sure, I've been at a party or two where someone was lighting up, and I learned to recognize the smell by Fiona's giggles and the stupid jokes Dax made about the skunky scent in the air. But I've never even been drunk, not really. I've sipped the beers that boys have handed me over the years, but I just didn't like the taste enough to drink much. I always thought that I'd get around to it later.

I never meant to become such a Goody Two-shoes. I'm not sure exactly when it happened. Right now, that seems beside the point. Because this little pill is the price of entry, and I've got to get inside. I'm not leaving Kensington without talking to Jas, that much I know for sure.

"Fine," I say, swiping the pill from his hand, which I can't help noticing is hot and clammy.

"All right," the boy says, grinning. He actually seems proud that he's done his job. "Let's get you hooked up."

"Do you have some water?" I ask, lifting the pill to my mouth.

"Nah," he says. "Kicks in faster if you chew it up anyway."

I bite into it and almost gag. "Tastes like shit," I say as a bitter flavor fills my mouth, the pill chalky and dense, sticking between my teeth. Maybe this is why they call it dust; it literally coats your mouth.

"Remember that taste for next time. It's how you know you're getting the real thing."

I shake my head. "There won't be a next time."

The kid laughs. "I've heard that before," he says, his voice fading into a singsong as he finally opens the door for me. "Just remember," he adds as I step inside the house, "only the first one's free."

Even though Jas's house is a mirror image of Pete's, this place doesn't look like anywhere I've ever been before. To begin with, there's the smell. It's like a physical assault: salt water and sand, smoke and liquor, sweat and skin, all lingering together into something else entirely, something hot and dark and overwhelming. Trying to take deep breaths only makes it worse.

The sliding doors that lead to the backyard are wide open; the yard is lit up like it's on fire. Floodlights, I realize. There's a

DJ spinning records behind the pool; he has strobe lights and steam machines. He must be using a generator; Jas must have this whole place running on generators, like we're survivors of some natural disaster.

From here I can see the pool, filled with cerulean water, brighter and bluer than the water crashing onto the beach below. People are floating through the pool fully dressed, in bathing suits; someone is even naked. They're dancing, making out, laughing.

The smell, the blinking lights, the pulsing music—they fill me up so that all I want to do is run away, back to the cliffs, back to Pete, where I was only aware of the ocean and our breath.

This place is a madhouse. No wonder drugs are the price of entry. Anything to quiet the sounds, to get some peace from the beat that's as steady and unrelenting as a pulse.

I try to imagine my brothers walking into one of these parties. Maybe, like me, they didn't come here looking to get high. Maybe, like me, they were willing to take a pill just to get inside. Maybe, like me, they never intended to take dust a second time. Maybe they just wanted to know what all the fuss was about.

I walk through the crowd to the very edge of the backyard, squeezing my way between hot bodies and cold sweat, stepping on cigarettes that are still burning on the dry grass—fires waiting to happen—skirting puddles of sticky alcohol from cups that have been dropped, forgotten, on the ground.

Maybe I can get out of here before the drug even kicks in. I'll keep to the edges, making an enormous circle around the party until I spot him. Methodical, like this is an assignment from a teacher. Find Jas and get an A. And I always get As.

I stick my hands into my pockets. I've never been good at parties. Never wanted to head for the dance floor or take shots of whatever cheap vodka had been snuck inside. Once, at a party on the beach last fall, I poured beer from my can when my date wasn't looking, just so that I'd be able to ask him to get me another can, and then another, and then another. By the end of the night, he thought I'd had more to drink than he had, and he couldn't stop talking about how high my tolerance must be. When I told Fiona, she thought it was hilarious. Dax thought it was a shame to waste all that beer.

It's hard to make out faces between flashes of the strobe lights. I gasp when someone trips, falling into the pool, but he resurfaces laughing, even though his lip is bleeding.

What does dust do, exactly? I shake my head, and as I do, the light from the floodlights seems to drag across my field of vision. I guess I'm about to find out.

My circle halfway complete, I stop behind the DJ's table, even though here the music is so loud I can't hear myself think. I stand on my tiptoes, craning my neck to see over bodies bouncing up and down with the beat. A shirtless boy carrying a skateboard looks like Michael from behind, but then he turns and I see his eyes are a dark, muddy brown—nothing like my brother's. I hear a laugh that sounds like John's, but I can't for the life of me find the person it's coming from.

Suddenly, the music stops—a break between songs, something even the worst DJs know to avoid. But I'm grateful for the silence, for the way the bodies stop dancing, for the stillness that allows me to look around in peace. There, directly opposite me, clear across the party, is Jas, leaning against the side of the house. He raises his eyebrows when he sees me staring, and I immediately drop my gaze, looking at his shoes—boots that peek out from under dark, tight jeans, standing out against the sea of flip-flops and sandals and bare feet.

The music starts up again, louder than before. When I look up, Jas is gone. Shit.

"Wow," I say, and the word feels sticky in my mouth, like I've just swallowed a spoonful of syrup. "Wow," I say again, slower this time, remembering what the boy at the door told me: take all the time you need.

All the time I need for what?

To find Jas, that's right. I smile. Wait, I was already smiling. I'm smiling so wide my jaw hurts, but then it doesn't hurt. The ache is sweet. I press my hands to my cheeks, soft as silk. Soft as a kiss. Even my teeth feel like satin.

I shake my head.

I'm looking for Jas. I'm looking for Jas. I'm looking for Jas.

"No need to shout, sugar," someone says.

I look up and see a boy wearing a T-shirt and board shorts, like almost everyone else here. He's got a beer bottle in one hand, and his other arm is slung around a bikini-clad girl. I didn't realize I was shouting. I didn't realize I was saying a word out loud.

"He's right over there," the boy says, pointing.

"Where?" I ask, following his finger with my gaze. There are those blue eyes again, bright even in the darkness. I wonder what it would be like to stand close to those eyes. Would it feel warm, like standing next to a fire, or cold, like standing beside an enormous block of ice?

Jas is right where I saw him, leaning against his house. Maybe he never moved. Slowly, careful not to blink—I don't want to lose sight of him again—I begin making my way across the back-yard to Jas. My feet feel fuzzy on top of the wooden porch—wait, when did I take my shoes off?—and then it feels like I'm weightless, like gravity stopped existing at all and there's noth-ing, not a thing, tethering me to the ground, and I'm floating toward the handsome boy with the dark jeans and the black boots. But without gravity, there wouldn't be any waves, and even with the music pounding in my ears, I can still hear the waves crashing against the beach below.

"Where are my brothers?" I shout, and Jas's blue eyes narrow in confusion. I say it again. I say their names. I say *Witch Tree*. Or maybe I don't say anything. It doesn't feel like my mouth is moving. I try again: *brothers, John and Michael, Witch Tree*. But the look on Jas's face doesn't change, doesn't shift with even the slightest hint of recognition. Instead, he reaches for me.

"Wendy, how much did you take, sweetheart?" He pulls me close, and his hands are cool against my skin, refreshing as rain.

I let myself be folded in against him, my back against his front. I close my eyes; it feels like Jas is going to take care of me, wrapped around me like a blanket. He smells delicious, like soap and salt water and beer.

"Don't worry, it'll wear off eventually," he says, whispering the words into the back of my hair, his breath soft and cool and soothing, his voice deep.

How does he know my name? I never told him my name. Wait, that's right, Belle told him my name. Belle, who knew my brothers, knew they were dusters. And Jas supplies the dusters.

"No," I say, shaking my head and disentangling myself from

him, even though the minute my body separates from his, I miss his touch. What the hell is in this drug that it makes me long to be close to the person who sold dust to my brothers?

"No," I repeat, more certain this time. I say the words again: *brothers, John and Michael, Witch Tree.* But this time, when Jas reaches for me, I manage to dance out of his reach. I can feel my face falling, crumbling up like it's made of paper and someone has thrown water on it.

Not water. Tears. I'm crying.

But the tears feel so good on my skin that soon I'm cooing like a baby.

"You can't catch me!" I shout, gleeful as a little kid playing tag. But then I trip, hitting the ground hard.

Jas steps forward, concern knitted into his brows, but I want to tell him it's okay. The fall didn't hurt. Even the gravel against my cheek feels good. I taste something I don't recognize, not at first. Blood. I must have bitten myself. It tastes as good as chocolate cake.

I stand up; it feels like I'm bouncing off the ground.

Jas reaches for me; I think maybe he's going to catch me, but I dart away. He reaches for me again, wrapping his arms around mine. The muscles in my shoulders ache deliciously, sore from all the paddling I did this afternoon. Was that just this afternoon? It seems like a million years ago.

There's no reason for me to stay here with Jas, not anymore. He doesn't even know what I'm talking about, doesn't even know my brothers' names. But I don't want to leave either. Not when everything here feels so good.

20

I'M NOT IN THE BACKYARD ANYMORE. I'M NOT anywhere. Or maybe I'm everywhere. Was my skin always this soft? There is a set of stairs beneath me. Not cool tiles like the floor at Pete's house on the cliffs or in the glass house on the hill. These stairs are soft and plush, and so hot I think they must be on fire.

Fire is so beautiful. Really, it travels in waves, just like the ocean.

I'm not alone. Someone is holding on to my waist, pulling me up, up, up over the hot stairs. Carpet. These stairs are covered in carpet.

"You're gonna be fine, Wendy," Jas says, his voice deep and rich. He's so close, I can still smell him.

Wait: it's quiet. So quiet. There's no music, no party. The house is awash with light: the sun is shining brightly through the windows. It's daytime. The party must have ended hours ago.

But not for me. I spin away, dancing in the sunlight, the carpet warm and soft beneath my feet. Funny that Jas's house is carpeted. Houses by the beach usually have bare floors. Carpets can be ruined by sand and salt too easily.

Jas laughs. "These new pills stay with you for a long time," he says.

I shake my head. What does he mean, these new pills? Oh, that's right, the dust. For some reason, this seems insanely funny, and I start laughing so hard that I think I'll never stop, so hard that I can feel my abdominal muscles wince at the effort of taking my next breath, but I can't stop.

Wendy Darling is not the kind of girl who takes drugs. Wendy Darling doesn't even stay out past curfew. But there's no curfew anymore, not where I live now, not with Pete in the house on the cliffs. In Pete's house, they can stay on the beach all night just to make sure that they're there when the waves peak first thing in the morning.

I shake my head. I don't live in the house on the cliffs anymore. Do I live here, with Jas? No. Jas is bad. I don't like Jas.

"I don't like you," I say, but there's still laughter in my voice. "It's all your fault," I add.

My words must surprise him, because he drops my arm, and the next thing I know, I'm running, running away from him. Out of his house and down stairs that are wooden and rickety, dirty and covered in sand. And then I feel the sand beneath my feet. I'm on the beach. The sun is shining yellow and red and pink on my back—wait, it's sunset, not sunrise, when did that happen? I have the whole beach to myself, and I spin around, spin around, dancing to music that only I can hear.

But then he is beside me again, dancing right along with me.

Why did he follow me here? Why won't he let me out of his sight?

"Come back to the house please, Wendy." And he says it so politely, so softly, with such a smile playing on the edges of his lips, that I say okay and let him lead me back up and over the cliffs. A cool breeze rises off the ocean, following us back to Jas's house, making me shiver.

I wonder just how long we were dancing on the beach, just how much time we've spent together. Wait, I've been on the beach with Jas before.

"What did you mean when you said I looked different?"

"What are you talking about, sweet girl?"

"On the beach. You said living in Kensington agrees with me."

Jas's teeth are so white when he smiles, I bet he scares the sharks.

"I meant that you looked beautiful, Wendy."

I laugh. What a funny word. "Bee-yoo-tee-full!" I shout, each syllable making me laugh harder.

I'm in a bed. The softest bed in the entire world, softer even than the bed in the house on Brentway. I start laughing again: did I really help rob a house? The sheets in this bed are cotton, but they're silky as satin, and the pillows are fluffy beneath my head. The room is dark, but my eyes are wide open. Suddenly, I'm thirsty, thirstier than I've ever been in my whole life. I open my mouth to ask for water, but my throat is too parched to say a word. But then I roll over and a tall glass of water is here on the floor beside the bed, waiting for me.

And sitting beside the glass, he is still there. Refilling my glass, offering me coffee and tea, crackers and Popsicles.

Oh my god, a Popsicle would be so delicious right now. How did he know that?

Well, of course he knows that. He knows exactly what a person high on dust would want. Which reminds me of why I came to him in the first place. Why I took this drug in the first place. I open my mouth to ask my questions, but instead of speaking, I'm coughing. He hands me another glass of water, so cold, so delicious, that I wonder why I ever wasted time drinking anything other than water in the first place.

I sit up. I stand. I shout question after question, and I swear I can see my words hitting Jas like bullets, sliding down his body like ink.

I drop the empty glass on the floor and collapse into the bed. His hand reaches out for me, brushing my hair away from my face. His touch feels so good. He drops his hand and slides across the floor, backing away from the bed, putting some distance between us. But he stays where I can see him, disappearing only to bring me more water, an orange-flavored Popsicle, a plate piled high with crackers and cookies.

Why is he still with me? Why does he care?

21

I WAKE UP ON THE GROUND.

I'm not supposed to be here. I'm supposed to be spending this summer at home, with my parents, shopping for towels and pillows to bring with me to Stanford in the fall. I'm supposed to be on the beach with Fiona, slathering on sunscreen while she sprays herself with tanning oil, watching from a distance while she and Dax splash hand in hand through the waves.

"This is all wrong," I say out loud, and my throat feels like it's on fire. I swallow, cringing at the sour taste in my mouth.

Someone is grabbing me. I turn toward the sensation, expecting to see Jas, but instead I see Fiona's face, hear Fiona's voice saying, "My god, Wendy, what happened to you?"

Even though she's standing right beside me, it sounds like she's miles away. She repeats her question, louder this time. She's in her pajamas, her eyes still cloudy with sleep. I must have woken her.

The scent of eucalyptus tells me where I am. I'm sitting on

Fiona's front porch; my fingers are still pressing her doorbell. I drop my hand into my lap. I'm shivering. How did I get here?

I close my eyes, willing myself to remember anything that happened over the past few days. I remember kissing Pete on the cliffs. I thought nothing had ever felt as good as those kisses; I thought nothing ever would.

But in a flash I remember Jas's party. Pete's kisses didn't even feel as good as falling to the ground felt when I was on dust.

I went to the party looking for answers about my brothers. Did I even remember to ask Jas about them? I don't know. I wonder if that's what happened to my brothers; if they simply forgot to come home after they took dust, if they simply forgot that my parents and I were back in the glass house waiting for them.

I remember running down the beach, the waves crashing in their perfect rhythm, one right after another, a surfer's paradise. I remember the shadow of someone else beside me. I remember reaching for Pete and finding Jas instead.

I let Fiona lift me off the ground and pull me into her house. My car is parked in the driveway beside us, but there's no way I could have driven it here, not in the state I'm in.

I may never stop crying. Sometimes it comes in choking, wracking sobs and sometimes it's silent tears streaming down my face and filling my throat with the taste of salt water.

I cry until I think there can't possibly be any water left in me for more tears, and then I cry some more.

Fiona's mother is standing just inside the doorway. She's wearing her bathrobe.

"Wendy?" she asks, like she's not sure it's really me. "What are you doing here?" She looks from me to Fiona, a dozen questions just waiting to be asked.

But before she can ask a single one, I ask one of my own.

"What time is it?"

"It's six in the morning," she answers.

"Exactly?"

She glances at a clock behind her. "Six-oh-seven," she says.

I actually stop crying for a second. That's how good it feels to know exactly what time it is.

Fiona whispers that I should go to her room. Even in my addled state, I know exactly how to get from the front door to Fiona's room; remember, from years of countless sleepovers, how much Fiona hates being woken up in the morning.

I climb into her bed, her pink sheets as familiar to me as my own. I wrinkle my nose because there is a smell here I don't recognize. Something new mixed in with Fiona's shampoo and the fancy detergent her housekeeper uses.

It's Dax, I realize with a start. Dax's smell is all over.

I nestle deep under her covers, letting myself be drenched in her scent and Dax's, too. Willing away the smells of Kensington, of the beach, of the ocean, of Pete, of Jas.

"Wendy," Fiona says slowly, "I'm calling your parents."

"No," I manage to get out between sobs. "Wait."

I really don't know why I'm crying like this. I've never been much of a crier. Maybe these tears are just a chemical reaction, some dip in my neurotransmitters from everything the drug used up. Everything it's still using up as it snakes its way through my system.

"I lied to you," I say carefully, struggling to hold my voice even. "I wasn't at a hotel all this time, grieving."

Fiona seems disappointed in me. "Where were you?" she asks carefully.

"I was looking for my brothers," I say, and then the flood-gates open. I tell her everything: about Kensington Beach, about the waves that flow like clockwork and the sand as soft as flour. I tell her about Jas and dust, and my brothers getting kicked out and leaving to surf Witch Tree, about cliffs and the tiles in the house that never got dirty. I even tell her about the party and the drug so powerful that it made lights bleed and pain a pleasure. I tell her about everything.

Everything but Pete. I don't make a decision to leave him out, not exactly. But when I tell the story, he just kind of stays out of it. Maybe I'm still too embarrassed that I fell for him when I should have known better.

While I speak Fiona holds my hand, and sometimes she stops to hug me. She nods when she should, her eyes widen when they should, they even brim with tears when I tell her that my broth-ers were hooked on drugs. When I finish, I say, "I know it sounds crazy. I know I must look crazy."

Fiona shakes her head warmly. "No," she says. "It all makes perfect sense."

I'm so grateful for her understanding that I begin crying again, and Fiona pulls me into a hug.

"You need to get some rest," she says soothingly. "Lie down. Go to sleep."

"I need some rest," I echo, remembering that I was up all

night. Fiona pulls the covers up around me like I'm a little kid and closes the door gently behind her.

Before it clicks shut, she says, "Everything's going to be okay."

I close my eyes and welcome sleep.

· · · · ·

I awake to whispers.

I don't know who Fiona is talking to, but whoever it is, she's telling them my story; telling them about Kensington Beach, and dust, and my brothers. I get up and open the door.

Fiona and my parents are standing in the hallway outside.

"Mom, Dad," I say, and they look at me sharply, sadly, almost guiltily, as though they were doing something to me behind my back. I try to ignore my pounding headache. "I'm sorry I didn't tell you right away. I thought I could handle it by myself. I was wrong, I know I was wrong. Did you call the police? Tell them to reopen the case? To head to Witch Tree, wherever that is?"

I try to smile, but my parents look so devastated that it's impossible.

"Wendy," my father says gently, "your brothers—"

"I know, I know. They're addicts. It's bad. But—"

"No," he says firmly. "No."

"I didn't want to believe it at first either."

"Wendy," he says again, "your brothers are dead."

I shake my head; they don't understand.

"Wendy. Your brothers died months ago. The police found their boards up the coast, destroyed."

I look at Fiona, desperately confused. "I thought you told them—"

"I did, Wendy, I did."

"But then—"

"Wendy—"

I shake my head. "You didn't believe me?"

"Wendy," Fiona says, "it makes perfect sense, like I said. We even called that grief counselor and she agreed. You're so torn up about the loss of your brothers that your brain constructed this, this . . ."

She searches for the words. Somewhere in this house, I know, is a pad of paper scrawled with notes they took while talking to the grief counselor.

Finally, she says, "This alternate reality to protect yourself from what really happened."

"I know what really happened," I say. My head is pounding so hard that I think I could dance in time to its rhythm.

"You have been taking drugs," my mother says, thin-lipped. "This is all some kind of psychosis."

"Is that what you told them?" I ask, turning back to Fiona. "Just because I was gone for a few weeks?"

Fiona shakes her head. "It started before you left. At the bonfire, the night we graduated. Even Dax thought you were acting strange—"

"Well if Dax thought so, it must be true. He knows me so well, after all," I spit.

Fiona bites her lip and looks at her feet. I turn to face my mother.

"Mom, you have to listen to me—"

She shakes her head. "We're going home."

I open my mouth to protest, to insist, to beg. But my mother looks so helpless, so defeated, so *empty*, that instead I just nod and follow my parents out the door. I even let Fiona hug me goodbye, when what I really want to do is scream at her, maybe even hit her for not believing me, for betraying me.

· · · · ·

Nana is waiting at the door, but she doesn't run to me the way she usually does when I come home. Instead, she backs away from me, wary, like she doesn't recognize me. Like I'm a stranger. I start crying all over again.

"I know, honey," my father says, coming up from behind me and putting an arm around my shoulder. "I know."

My mother carries my duffel bag in from the car—I don't even remember bringing it with me from Pete's house, but I must have—unzips it on the kitchen counter, and begins sifting through it like she's looking for contraband. It takes me a second to realize that she's looking for drugs.

"Mom," I say, "there's nothing bad in there. Just clothes and some extra cash." She won't even look at me, just keeps going through my bag.

"Why don't you go to your room, honey?" my father says finally.

"Am I being punished?"

"Of course not."

"Then why are you sending me to my room?"

He sighs. "Because that's what they told us to do. Something about reestablishing authority."

I shake my head. I wonder if my parents would even have

noticed that I was gone if I hadn't come back in the state I'm in. If I weren't aching with withdrawal, I think a tiny part of me would be glad that they're paying attention. Even though they're wrong—about me, about my brothers, about Kensington—they seem to have begun to come out of the fog they've been living in for the last nine months.

"Who told you to do that?"

"The people at the center."

"What center?"

"It's for people with problems like yours."

No one has problems like mine, I think but do not say.

He continues, "Supposed to be the best in the country. They'll admit you just as soon as a spot opens up."

As soon as a spot opens up.

He doesn't offer me any further explanation—will it be days, weeks, months? Will I still be allowed to start college in September? I want to ask, but I can feel my pulse pounding beneath my temples, and I'm pretty sure that if I open my mouth again nothing but sobs will come out.

I have to beg Nana to follow me into my room, and even once inside, she keeps her distance from me. I can't say I blame her. I catch a glimpse of my face in the mirror; I don't look anything like myself. I can't say exactly what about me has changed; my hair is the same color, my eyes the same shape. My skin is tanner, I suppose. There's something else, something deeper that's changed. I still look like me, but off somehow. Like I've aged ten years in a few days.

Or maybe it's just that I've cried so much that my face has been emptied out, dry and salty as a desert.

22

I DON'T KNOW HOW MUCH TIME GOES BY BEFORE
the pain sets in. Something beyond the headache and past the
tears, an ache from somewhere deep inside my chest that radiates into my joints so that I can't turn my neck or grip a pencil.
I want to cry out, but I don't want to make Nana more frightened of me than she already is. And it's not like I want my parents to come running.

How can it hurt this much? I only used the drug once. No
wonder my brothers went back to Jas and asked for more. No wonder Pete couldn't convince them to stop.

Suddenly, I'm breathtakingly, teeth-chatteringly cold. This is
what people mean when they say their blood runs cold. This is a
cold that's coming from *inside* of me, as though my very bones
are turning to ice. I burrow under my covers, an animal hiber-
nating her way through the cold winter.

But my sleep is fitful, and when I dream it is always, always
of Kensington. I see Belle on the water, flying over a wave as

though she has wings—sometimes she does have wings—and soon I can't remember whether I ever did see her surf or just dreamed I did. She's so tiny, after all; surely if she'd tried to surf, the ocean would have swallowed her whole. Like they say it did my brothers.

I dream of—or do I simply remember?—sitting on the handlebars of a bike as it flies down a hill, slipping inside a mansion door. That must have been a dream. I would never have done that in real life.

I dream about a house with tiles so white they seem to glow in the moonlight, of boys who come back from the beach but don't track a single grain of sand through the house. I dream of waves that come in perfect sets, with symmetry and grace that would dumbfound the scientists who insist that perfection doesn't exist in nature. I dream of sand so soft and sunlight so warm, but I wake up shivering in sheets damp with sweat.

I dream of being held by a tall form with beautiful eyes, whose skin is dry and whose breath is cool as winter, whose voice sounds like rain. I dream that he takes flight over the waves on a surfboard, as though the board is just some extension of his feet, a part of his body.

Or maybe I'm not dreaming. Maybe I'm just tossing and turning all night long. Or maybe it's day. It's so hard to tell here, in the glass house that never really gets dark.

And I dream of a boy named Pete, tall and skinny and covered in freckles. A boy who always looks like he's laughing because of the tan lines that wink out from the corners of his eyes. A boy into whose hand my own fits perfectly, a boy whose laugh sounds like the call of a crow heralding the morning. A boy who held me against his chest and promised to help me. A boy who led me into the ocean and helped me fly.

I'm never sure if he's a memory or a dream. My parents keep telling me it was all a hallucination. When she searched my bag, my mother took my notebook away, the one where I wrote down all my research.

I search my sheets for sand, but I find none. I don't know why I expect to find sand in my bed—I haven't been to the beach in weeks, haven't even left the house since coming home. But every morning, I wake up disappointed. My mother thinks she's helping me when she strips the bed and washes the sheets almost every day. Neither of us understands why I cry every time I slip between the freshly laundered sheets, sheets without a trace of the sea left on them, not even a whisper of the ocean; only detergent and a hint of my mother's perfume.

"It's gone," I whisper.

"What's gone, honey?" I look up at her; her eyes are so sad and far away, narrowed with concern.

I shake my head. "Maybe it was never there to begin with."

"That's right, honey," she says, and I try not to think about the wrinkles around *her* eyes, the way they've deepened from so much crying. Just the opposite of the boy's eyes, the lines around them that make it look like he's smiling. Even when I'm yelling at him. Which, apparently, I did, just before I left him.

Why does missing these people and that place ache like a withdrawal all its own? Every night, my dreams are filled with Pete and even Jas, images so vivid and so powerful that I think they, at least, *must* be a memory.

Because if they're not real, then how do I miss them so much?

. . . . .

And then suddenly, one morning, the pain is gone. I wake up hungry. My stomach clenches food like a vise, and I think I'll never be sick again. I practically skip to the shower and wash my hair three times, lather up soap over my skin until it looks like I'm covered in foam.

Pete told me once that surfers can breathe in the oxygen from the foam that crests on the edge of waves when they're being pummeled and can't quite make it to the surface. They call it soup, he said.

The memory comes like a flash of lightning and disappears just as quickly. I shake my head and wash my hair a fourth time. I'm sick of smelling like my bed, like cold sweats, sour with illness. I want to look and smell like myself again, want Nana to stop eyeing me warily, like I'm some kind of impostor in her best friend's skin. When I get out of the shower, I start a load of laundry. I turn on my computer and find e-mail after e-mail from Stanford, briefing me on orientation, telling me that my dorm is called Branner Hall and my roommate's name is Sadie. There's a list of suggested items to bring, everything from extra towels to flashlights, and I print it. My mother and I can drive to the store later, get everything on this list and then some. I feel like a little kid who's about to start first grade, eager to fill her backpack with school supplies.

I spend the next few days normally: driving to the mall with my mother, laughing during visits with Fiona. Once, I ask if Fiona and I can drive down to the beach, and my parents look slightly panicked until Fiona breaks in and says she'd rather not go. She's been avoiding the sun this summer, she says, even though her tan belies her words. Some aunt of hers was diagnosed with skin cancer, she claims. Instead, we watch movies and my father picks up Chinese.

My parents seem almost back to normal; my father is going into the office regularly, and my mother gets dressed almost every day. Sadness still hangs over the house, but it feels lighter somehow, less likely to shatter the windows and walls. Maybe this is all for my benefit; maybe my parents think it's their fault I went crazy, because they were so intent on their own loss that they forgot to pay attention to mine. It's kind of a relief to have my parents back, despite everything else.

On a Wednesday afternoon, my father knocks politely on my door, bringing a blast of cold air along with him into the room. I've opened my windows to let dry California air fill my room, despite the heat of the day. The rest of the house is locked shut and filled with artificially cooled air.

"Hey, Dad," I say, holding a new list out in front of me; I can't stop making lists of school supplies, last-minute things to do. "Think Mom's up for a trip to Bed Bath & Beyond today?"

He looks at the list like it's gibberish and looks at me like I'm speaking Greek.

"Come on, I've only got a few weeks left to stock up." It only just occurred to me to check the date this morning. Technically, it's six weeks, since Stanford starts in mid-September.

"Wendy," he says gently. I'm sitting at my desk, and he walks toward me until he's standing over me. My father is not a tall man, but I shrink beneath his shadow nonetheless. "I know this stuff has messed with your memory, but surely you remember—"

"Remember what?"

"They called us from Montana," he says. "A few days ago."

"What's in Montana?"

"The center."

Slowly I lower myself onto my bed. They're still sending me there? I honestly thought they'd have been over it by now. I'm back to normal. Even Nana is back to sleeping in my bed with me, nuzzling close, covering me in kisses. *"Montana?"*

He nods.

"Dad, I'm fine. It was just that one time. Surely you guys can see that by now?"

My father shakes his head. "They told us this place is the best."

"Who told you?"

"We did a lot of research for you, honey. We wanted to find the best possible place for you."

What kind of research could they have possibly done? They've never even heard of dust, so how would they know which is the best place for rehabilitation from it? Unless they think that the drug is just another of my hallucinations—and of course, they do. They must think I was on something else, something they've heard of, something they've seen covered on the news.

"The best possible place for me is *here*," I say, beginning to sweat. "If you want, I'll talk to a therapist here."

He's staring out my window, a sad but hardened expression on his face.

"Look at me, Dad," I say, trying desperately to keep my voice from shaking. "Look how much *better* I am."

My father shakes his head. "Your hallucinations still have a hold on you. At night, you're still having dreams—"

"How do you know?"

"You shout in your sleep. A name, a place. I don't know."

"Whose name?" John, I think, or Michael.

"Pete. Every night, you shout for someone named Pete. Wendy, who's Pete?"

I shake my head. "I don't remember," I say finally. It's not exactly a lie.

23

MY EYES FLUTTER OPEN IN THE MIDDLE OF THE night. The scent of him—salt water and Tide, blue eyes and beer—fills my room. I must be dreaming. But it's Pete's name they say I've been calling in my sleep, not *his*.

My windows are still open, my room cool now, after hours without sunlight. The only sound is a tapping on the glass; I look to my windows, expecting to see nothing but the night-lights shining up from the city, but instead there's a boy scratching at the glass like a cat asking to be let inside, a boy tall and muscular, pressing my window open even wider and climbing into my room. Beside me on the bed, Nana stiffens. I expect her to bark, growl, maybe even lunge at the intruder. But she must like the smell of him, because she hops off the bed and greets him with one of her enormous kisses.

I'm not about to do the same. Not to the man whose drugs kept me sick for weeks, who's the reason behind my parents' crazy idea to send me away, the reason my brothers got kicked out of Pete's house, a home I still think of as a safe place, even after everything that's happened.

I do get out of bed and run past him to the window, looking for a ladder, a rope, a bunch of bedsheets tied together. How did he get up here? Our house is perched on a steep hill and made of glass. There's not exactly much to hang on to.

When he speaks, his voice is deep, as though strained from years of swallowing sand and salt water.

"Wendy" is all he says. The sheepishness in his voice is hard to reconcile with his laser-sharp eyes. Or with the fact that he just scaled a wall and climbed into my bedroom.

"What are you doing here?"

"I needed to talk to you."

"Ever heard of a phone?"

"I didn't exactly have your number."

I nod, backing away from him, tripping over Nana and almost falling into my bed.

"What did you want to talk to me about?"

"Do you remember what you said that night?"

I shake my head, sitting down. Immediately I wish that I'd sat at my desk and not on my bed. Sitting on my bed while Jas is in the room feels too intimate.

"I don't remember much at all. It comes to me sometimes, in flashes, but I can't quite put it together."

"That sounds like you. Trying to figure things out like a puzzle."

I'm taken aback. "How do you know what sounds like me?" I ask.

"We spent some time together, Wendy."

"Yeah, well, I wasn't exactly myself then." I pause. "How long exactly?" I've never been able to quite figure out just how many days I spent lost on dust before I found myself in Fiona's driveway.

"About two days. You were so far gone that you didn't fall asleep once," Jas answers, and I'm surprised that he doesn't hesitate, doesn't try to sugarcoat.

"What about you?"

"Me?"

"Did you sleep?"

He shakes his head. "Someone had to keep an eye on you."

"How did I end up at my friend's house?"

"On the second morning, you asked me to take you home. We were about halfway here when you started panicking."

"About what?"

"Some lie you'd told your parents. You said you were supposed to have been with Fiona. So I left you there, with your car. Hitchhiked my way back to Kensie."

I nod.

As though he understands, Jas adds, "Even high on dust, you were worried about the truth. Never saw that before."

"My brothers weren't quite so concerned with honesty?" I spit out accusingly.

Jas shakes his head sadly. "You talked a lot about your brothers when you were in my house," he says.

"I did?"

He nods, still smiling. "Well, maybe not talked. You shouted about them, mostly."

"That doesn't sound like me."

"Like you said, you weren't quite yourself."

I bristle. "Thanks to you. Your cover charge."

His smile vanishes. "I'm sorry," he says. "People who come to that party know what they're getting into, usually."

"Do they know about the withdrawal?" Even though I've felt better for a long time, my room still has a hint of illness to it, like the scent of my sickness saturated the walls.

Jas doesn't answer. At least he doesn't lie.

Finally, he says, "I think I can help you find your brothers."

"What?" I ask, sitting up straighter.

"I knew them," he says, running his hands through his hair, pacing the length of my room like an animal in a cage that's two sizes too small for him. His skin practically glows in the lights coming in from the city.

I sit on my hands.

"I knew them, they were regulars. Up until a few months ago—January, I think."

"January," I echo. That's when Matt said Pete kicked the boys out.

"I honestly hadn't given them a second thought until you came to my party, shouting their names, and shouting about Witch Tree."

"Belle said that when they left, they told her they were headed there."

Jas nods. "It broke early this winter. It's a winter wave—most of the big ones up and down the coast here are."

"So they wouldn't be there now is what you're telling me? They'd be long gone?"

Jas shakes his head. "Normally, yeah. But a big northwest

swell is brewing off the coast of Oregon. Never happened before, not this time of year. Surfers from all over the world are coming."

My pulse quickens. "Including my brothers?"

Jas shrugs. "I can't promise you that. But they might be. And I . . ." He pauses, stops pacing, and looks at me. "I know more than just the best places to surf up the coast, Wendy. I know the right places to look for—"

I finish his sentence for him, "The right places to look for kids who might be looking for other things."

At least he doesn't seem proud to be such an expert.

"The wave won't break again until winter, if it breaks again at all this year," he says. "None of these big waves will. That much I can tell you for sure. I don't know when you'll get another chance like this."

Silence hangs between us while I consider his words. "Why are you here?" I ask finally.

Jas blinks; when his eyes are closed, the room seems to grow darker. "I told you. Because I think I can help you."

"Yeah, but why do you care about helping me?"

Jas hesitates before answering. "I can tell you're not going to give up until you find them," he says finally.

"How can you tell? Just because you spent a few days with me when I was high as a kite doesn't mean you know me."

Jas nods. "When you talked about them you got that same look on your face that you got when you were deciding to take your next wave."

I shake my head. "How do you know what I look like when I take a wave?"

He pauses, then looks almost sheepish when he answers. "I watched you. In the mornings. When you'd go out there and surf by yourself."

"You watched me?"

"Just in case. You know, you were a beginner, and no one else was around. I just wanted to make sure you were okay."

I should feel violated. The guy was *spying* on me every morning when I thought I was alone, every time I took my board out while Pete, Belle, and the rest of the boys slept. But I don't; instead, I'm kind of glad he was there. At least he didn't try to stop me, didn't run down the beach and tell me I shouldn't be surfing all alone, shouldn't try for the bigger waves, ought to wait for the gentler ones. And I'm glad that he knows something about me that no one else knows: I had the courage to take wave after wave all by myself.

Suddenly, Jas says, "I'm sorry about your brothers, Wendy. When I sold them the dust . . . I mean, I never meant for them to go missing."

"As opposed to all the kids you sell dust to who go right back home to their mothers?" I ask. Something about his coming here has emboldened me. I should be scared of him. But I'm not. And much to my surprise, he blushes under my gaze.

"Come with me," he says finally. "Let me help your brothers. Let me help you."

I open my mouth to ask about all the other dusters who need to be rescued, but he speaks before I can say another word.

"Please," he whispers.

· · · · ·

Nana didn't so much as bark when I followed Jas out the window, climbed onto his back, and slid down the side of the glass house. And I didn't so much as blink when I climbed into the truck Jas was washing in his driveway the day I met him, the flatbed now filled with surfboards and a Jet Ski tied down with bungee cords.

I couldn't say no to his invitation, not really. Staying home meant going to Montana, landlocked a million miles away from the ocean, from Kensington Beach, and maybe from my brothers, too. Yes, this guy is a drug dealer; who knows how much money he's made off of selling dust to unsuspecting kids, getting them hooked, ruining lives—if not ending them? A lot, I think, judging from the quality of this truck, the number of boards in the flatbed behind us.

But he's offered to help, and I'm not about to refuse.

Sitting as far from Jas as possible, my body pressed against the passenger-side door, I close my eyes and let a memory wash over me—a *memory*, I'm certain this time, not a dream: Pete's chin resting in the small of my back as we paddle out to take a wave. The board sticky with wax beneath me as I pull myself up to stand. The ocean dropping out below us as the board slides into place beneath the crest of the wave. And the sensation that I'm flying, weightless and carefree, with no one on the planet except Pete and me, no one else who knows exactly what this feels like.

I open my eyes. Jas is driving fast and the ocean's to our left and I can hear the waves, wide awake in the middle of the night.

Reality has never been so crystal clear.

24

WE'VE DRIVEN ABOUT FIFTEEN MINUTES WHEN JAS starts talking. "So tell me about your brothers anyway."

I shake my head, still hoping to gather clues. "You saw them more recently than I did. You tell me about them."

He ignores me. "You must really love them, to be searching so hard."

"I'm their big sister," I say. "It's not a question of how much I love them. I just . . ."

"It's just your job," Jas finishes for me, and I nod.

"Do you have any siblings?" I ask. I try to imagine him with a family, but it's impossible to see him any way but the way he is now, a drug-dealing surfer chasing his next wave.

"Not exactly," he nonanswers. "Tell me about growing up with John and Michael." When I'm silent, he adds, "It's a long drive in the middle of the night, Wendy. Think of it as helping to keep me awake."

Fine. I can just pretend that I'm talking to someone else.

"They always seemed twice my size, even though I was the older sister." I pause, smiling. "John had a way of talking down to me that made me feel like I was the baby in the family."

Jas laughs; his laugh is deep, and the car seems to vibrate with it.

"He was kind of a brat actually," I continue, laughing just a little bit myself. "They both were. You should have seen them on the beach. They'd take on any wave they wanted, waves that the kids twice their size shied away from. Once, Michael actually picked a fight with some surfers—like, grown-up surfers—claiming that one of them had cut him off on his way into a wave. I thought he was going to punch the guy in the face, if only he could have reached his face."

"What happened?"

I shrug. "I don't really know. By the end of the day, he was surfing right alongside them, picking up pointers from them left and right. Maybe that had been his plan all along."

"Sounds like they were pretty fearless."

I shake my head. "No, actually. I mean, yeah, they were fearless on the beach. But at home—whole different story."

"What were they scared of?"

I close my eyes, remembering. "They were scared of the dark. Once, we played hide-and-seek—the two of them against me—and they hid in a closet and got themselves locked inside. The closet is literally the only place in our house where it gets really pitch-dark."

"How old were they?"

"Four? Five?" I'm surprised I don't remember exactly. I do remember the sound of their voices yelling for me and the way I teased them through the door for giving up the game. I remember reaching for the doorknob to shout that I'd found them, and I remember that no matter how hard I turned the knob, the door just wouldn't open. I remember crying for my parents to come and save them. Later, when my father finally rescued them, prying the door off its hinges, my brothers blamed me for having gotten trapped in the first place.

That night was the first time my mother told us that the city lights were our own private night-lights. Even though they were mad at me, John and Michael slept in my room.

"What else?" Jas asks.

"Hmm?" I'm getting sleepy. I wouldn't have thought I'd be able to sleep—not beside this stranger, not with the adrenaline that began coursing through my veins the minute he stepped foot inside my room. But my voice feels cottony in my mouth; I shift in my seat, leaning my cheek against the leather of my headrest.

"What else were they scared of?" Jas prompts.

"The usual stuff. Earthquakes. Fire. I made fun of them for it once; they were eleven. How could they be so fearless on the water and so scared on land?"

"Sounds like the things that scared them didn't exist on the water."

"What do you mean?" I ask. My eyelids feel like they weigh a thousand pounds.

"You don't have to worry about earthquakes and fire on the water."

"What about the dark? It gets dark out there."

"Yeah, but they always surfed when the sun was shining, didn't they?"

I nod, remembering something Pete said about feeling more at home on the water than on dry land. "I guess."

"How old were they when they started surfing?"

"Ten."

"Lucky."

"How old were you?"

Jas doesn't answer, so I try another question. "How did you learn? My parents got the boys lessons, but they blew them off pretty fast."

Jas takes his eyes off the road to look at me. "Why do you want to know so much about me?"

"Why not? Like you said, it's a long drive in the middle of the night. You have to keep *me* awake, too."

Jas laughs. "Just haven't really thought about my past in a long time. Sometimes I think I can't really remember my life before I started surfing."

I nod sleepily; I bet John and Michael would say the same thing.

They hated the lessons my parents bought them. Hated learning technique on the dry sand when they ached to dive into the ocean. Still, they couldn't deny that they learned a lot that came in handy later. The lessons were expensive; maybe Jas's family wouldn't have been able to afford them. Maybe that's why he began dealing. Maybe that's when he moved to Kensington, when he met Pete, when the war between them began. Maybe after maybe fills my head, and all these questions I'm too tired to ask.

My eyelids grow so heavy that it's impossible to keep them open. I try for a while, blinking one eye open and then the next, but eventually, sleep wins out.

·　·　·　·　·

I wake up in an empty car. I'm in a parking lot. I unclick my seat belt and turn around and see a flashing sign that says VACANCY. A motel. I pull my phone from my purse. It's 4:14 a.m. We've been driving for three hours. There's no way we could have gotten to Witch Tree in only three hours.

I look up from my phone; Jas is walking from the motel lobby toward the car. When he sees me looking at him, he smiles.

"Morning," he says, opening my door for me. "Come on."

"Where?" I want to say *I'm not going anywhere with you*, but why would he believe that, seeing as I've already come this far with him?

"I got us a room. You fell asleep a couple hours ago, and I can only keep myself awake for so long."

"Aren't you used to pulling the occasional all-nighter?" I ask, thinking of the nights he stayed awake with me as I hop down from the truck.

Jas lifts my duffel bag from the back and slings it over his shoulder as easily as if it's filled with air. He doesn't answer me, just begins walking toward the motel. It's only two stories high, and Jas walks along the first floor, past darkened windows. I wonder if the lights are off because the people inside are sleeping or because the rooms are empty. Ours is almost the only car in the parking lot, and I'm pretty sure we're in the middle of no-where, though it's hard to tell at this hour.

I follow Jas up the stairs to the second floor, breathing deeply. Wherever we are, we're close to the ocean. I can smell the seaweed, feel the salt air on my skin. The outdoor hallway is barely lit, but I still can see the sand all over the floor. And I hear the sound of the ocean, the waves barreling against the shore, just a stone's throw away.

"Where are we?" I say to Jas's back.

He answers without turning around: "Halfway to Witch Tree."

"Witch Tree," I mutter. "Who would name a wave Witch Tree?"

"There's a dead cypress tree at Pescadero Point," Jas says, still not facing me. "You can see it from the water. A witch tree."

"Well, who would want to surf underneath a witch's tree?"

Now Jas does stop and turn around. "You want to surf where the waves are, Wendy. It's as simple as that." He looks so serious that it makes me blush. I have to will myself not to break eye contact with him. "You'd like Maverick's better. A wave near Half Moon Bay."

"Why?"

"Legend has it Maverick's was named after a dog."

I smile despite myself. "Really?"

"Yup. In the sixties, some guys were surfing there, and one of them brought his dog, who was named Maverick. Apparently, the dog was used to swimming out with the guys, so even though they left him onshore, he kept trying to catch them. But the conditions were too rough for him, so finally his owner had to tie him up back onshore. They called it Maverick's, and the name stuck."

Jas's deep voice takes on a sweet timbre when he talks about the dog swimming after his owner and I smile, trying to imagine what Nana would do if she saw me swimming into the sea, facing down forty-, fifty-, sixty-foot waves. Of course she'd come after me. She'd want to be beside me, whatever the adventure. I wish she could be with me now. Suddenly, I'm terribly homesick.

Jas resumes walking.

"What kind of dog was Maverick?" I ask suddenly.

"A white German shepherd," he answers.

"How do you know?"

Jas shrugs, the muscles in his back visible even through his T-shirt. "I don't remember a time when I didn't know that story," he says, sounding wistful.

He stops in front of a door marked *30*. As he fits the rusted key into the lock, my heart begins to pound. Am I really going to follow this stranger—no, worse than a stranger, because I know the things he's done—into a dark motel room in the middle of nowhere? Even if he did show up and offer to help me find my brothers? Even if he did drive all this way in the middle of the night while I slept at his side?

He surprises me by turning to me before he opens the door. "Don't worry," he says, "I got us a room with two beds."

I nod. I begin to say thank you, but then change my mind; he hasn't earned my thanks. Not yet.

25

I DON'T EXPECT TO SLEEP SOUNDLY WITH JAS IN the room, but I do. For the first night since I got back from Kensington, I don't wake up in sheets soaked with dream-sweat. Instead, I wake up gently when the sunlight pours in through the windows. I glance at my phone; I slept with it under my pillow, just in case. I'm not sure exactly what I thought might happen. It's after ten a.m. I roll over, expecting Jas to be snoozing in the bed across the room, but his bed is empty, his sheets barely wrinkled, almost as if he never went to sleep at all.

My parents will be awake by now. They will have discovered that I'm gone. There are five missed calls on my phone. They've probably called Fiona. Maybe they've called the police. Maybe they're blaming themselves. Maybe they're too frantic to do anything but pace the house, wondering where I've disappeared to now. I can't call the house; they'd ask too many questions if they heard my voice on the other end of the line.

Feeling guilty, I send my parents a text, just to let them know that I'm okay and I'll be back soon. Once the message is sent, I turn off my phone.

I don't bother getting dressed. I don't even put on shoes. I head out in my pajama bottoms and the T-shirt I slept in. It's breezy outside; the sun is shining, but the air feels heavy, ominous, as though the sky could crack open at any moment. Of course, I realize. A storm is coming, like Jas said. You can't have big waves without a storm coming eventually.

I'm not surprised when I see his truck in the parking lot, exactly where he left it last night. One of his boards is missing. He's on the beach. I think I knew that the instant I woke up.

These are not good waves, even I can see that. Small and choppy, with almost no curl to their lips when they peak. But Jas is making the most of them, turning and swishing his board over the chop, riding the lip of the wave, spinning like a ballet dancer and crouching like a tiger. He sees me watching him and waves at me, letting the current bring him back to shore.

"You didn't have to stop," I say as he walks toward me, balancing his board on his hip.

"Good morning to you, too." He plants the board in the sand.

"Right," I say, shaking my head. "Good morning."

"You sound surprised," he says, shaking the salt water out of his hair. Wet, it looks jet-black.

"Surprised?"

"You know, that a lowlife drug dealer like me has such good manners."

I blush, folding my arms across my chest. Jas has a gift for making me feel like I'm the bad guy. And maybe I am; he didn't owe me anything and yet he came to my window last night and brought me here.

"Even people like me have parents, you know. Mine taught me to say please and thank you, same as yours."

I don't answer. It's hard to believe that his childhood could have been anything like mine.

"Come here," Jas says, walking down the beach, his back to the motel. "I want to show you something."

I follow. Sand sticks to the bottom of my pajama pants, and the wind whips through my T-shirt, making me shiver. This beach is tiny; only a few yards from here the water meets the mountains, the hills dotted with houses. No doubt the owners paid premium prices for the views: ocean on one side, mountains on the other.

Jas stops walking and points to the biggest house by far, perched on the tallest peak. Three times the size of the glass house, at least. You could fit Jas's entire Kensington house inside of it. But unlike the other houses on the hill, it doesn't have enormous walls of windows facing the sea. Just normal-sized windows peeking out from beneath the Spanish tile roof, as though whoever built it didn't value the view at all.

"You see that house?" Jas asks.

"It's impossible not to see that house," I say. "Can you imagine all the trees they had to chop down to build that house? The roads they had to carve into the mountain just to get there?"

Jas nods. "I can imagine," he says. "I spent my whole childhood imagining."

I squint in the sunlight, holding up my hand to shield my eyes. "What do you mean?"

"That's where I grew up," he says.

"*That's* where you grew up?" I echo, wishing I didn't sound quite so incredulous, but Jas just laughs.

"Oh yes," he answers. "And I learned a lot more than my pleases and thank-yous. I learned just how to hold a salad fork and a steak knife, how to sip soup and drink iced tea every afternoon at four p.m. on the button."

I can't imagine that Jas lived a single second of his life on the button.

"How did you get from there to—" I stop myself, but Jas still answers the unasked question.

"I discovered surfing. It was impossible *not* to discover surfing. I could see every beach for miles around from that monstrosity, and every day, rain or shine, there they were. Surfers. Kids who had nothing but the clothes on their backs and the boards at their feet. Kids who were having a hell of a lot more fun than I was. So one morning, I snuck out, bought a board with my allowance, and . . ." He trails off, a strange sort of smile dancing on his lips at the memory. It's a look I know well; I've seen it on Pete's face and on my brothers' faces, too. That look that says you don't understand what the rest of us are doing on land, when there's that much joy to be found on the water.

"What happened?"

Jas shrugs. "It's not a particularly unique kind of story," he says. "I blew off school to chase waves. Rigged a rack to the roof of my car, strapped on a couple boards, and took off for days at a time. I wasn't exactly the son they had in mind—you know, straight As, college-bound, that kind of thing."

I nod, thinking about my brothers. By the time they ran away last year, they'd been driving my parents crazy for months. Every morning, when my parents and I woke up, we didn't know whether John and Michael would be home or would have vanished to hit up the newest beach where the waves were said to be charging. My parents came to dread phone calls most evenings from our school, warnings that if things didn't change my brothers would be held back a year, suspended, expelled. I got used to the way my mother's lips pressed into a thin line when my father lectured the boys about *priorities*. I got used to the look on my brothers' faces, like my dad didn't have a clue what that word really meant.

"When I was sixteen," Jas continues, "my parents said they were sending me away to school. I can't remember the name of the place, but it was someplace landlocked, nowhere near the ocean. They thought all I needed to get straightened out was some time on dry land." He laughs now, but there's no joy in it. "So I left. I wasn't scared of being homeless, of being alone with nothing but the clothes on my back and the board at my feet. But I was *terrified* of living a life without the ocean right outside my door."

I open my mouth to make a crack about a big tough guy like him being so frightened, but I press my lips together before a single word can escape. Because he looks so serious. He wasn't a big tough guy, not back then. He was a teenager, a kid. Like my brothers. Like me; and I've fled, too.

"A few months after I left, I ran into Pete. Little brat cut me off on a wave down on Huntington Beach." He smiles at the memory. "I charged after him like a bat out of hell. I mean it, I was ready to kick the kid's teeth in." He shakes his head. "But then he grinned at me and held out his hand. And before I knew it, I was crashing on the floor of whatever empty abandoned house he'd found to shack up in that week."

I smile. "Sounds kind of nice," I say.

Jas nods. "It was. It was . . ." He pauses. "Don't make fun of me for what I'm about to say, okay?"

I nod.

"It was the happiest time in my life. Pete and I just made our way up and down the coast, talking a big game, sleeping on couches and camping on beaches and just—surfing, you know? Every wave we could find.

"Finally, Pete discovered Kensington and those empty houses, and we moved into one of 'em and woke up with the sunrise to surf every morning. And we were so good. We *knew* how good we were. It was only a matter of time, we said, before we'd fly off around the world and start in on the big waves, the famous ones. At night, we'd say their names like other people say their prayers: Maverick's, Witch Tree, Jaws, Pipeline, Teahupoo."

"Cho-poo?" I echo. "What's that?"

"It's a wave in Tahiti," he explains. "*Teahupoo* is Tahitian for 'broken skulls.'"

"Seriously? You wanted to surf a wave called Broken Skulls?"

"I still want to," Jas says solemnly.

"Well then, why didn't you?" I ask. "Why didn't you and Pete get out there and conquer the world just like you planned?"

Instead of answering me, Jas begins walking back in the direction of the motel. I follow. "You hungry?" he says. "Let's get something to eat."

"I'm in my pajamas," I say. "I don't have any shoes on."

"Neither do I," Jas answers. "Don't worry, the place I'm taking you doesn't exactly have a 'no shoes, no shirt, no service' policy."

· · · · ·

"You see," Jas begins about twenty minutes later, when we're sitting at a splintered, beat-up picnic table that I think may have been painted white about fifty years ago, "my life used to be a lot like your life."

"Oh, did you make a habit of running off with drug dealers in search of your missing siblings, too?"

Jas shakes his head. "Let me rephrase that. My life used to be a lot like your life *used* to be. Fancy house on a hill—"

"My house is not like your house," I interrupt. My house is nice and all, but Jas grew up in a castle.

"Fair enough," he says, nodding. "But we both grew up in nice homes with parents who wanted what they thought was best for us. I went to school five days a week, just like you. I was supposed to go to college, just like you. I even dated a girl like you—smart, pretty, determined as hell to get the things she wanted, whether it was her next wave or her next test score."

"What happened to her?"

Jas smiles sadly. "Eventually she figured out that I wasn't one of the things she wanted."

I'm surprised at the heavy ache in his voice. "Broke your heart?"

Jas shrugs heavily. "She did the right thing, breaking up with me. She was still on the right track, and I had run off the rails.

Anyway, there're all different kinds of heartbreaks," he says slowly. "But you know that already, don't you?"

I nod, thinking of Fiona. A few days before graduation, she had called me crying. Dax had said that maybe they should break up before they went off to their separate colleges. She'd said he was breaking her heart just by thinking that, and I said all the things she needed to hear: *Of course he loves you. He doesn't really want to break up with you. Of course you can stay together, even at different schools.*

But really, I was thinking that my brothers broke my heart the instant they ran away. They broke our parents' hearts, too. I lived in a glass house full of shattered hearts and I hadn't even fallen in love yet.

But now, my heart feels better than it has in a long time. Maybe it's putting itself back together, getting stronger the closer I get to finding my brothers. Or maybe it's something else, someone else. I shake my head, blinking, decide to change the subject.

"You were going to tell me why you and Pete didn't go around the world together like you planned."

Jas nods, smiling at the waitress, who brings him a cup of coffee and places two plates of scrambled eggs in front of us.

"I didn't order scrambled eggs," I say.

"That's all they have here," Jas answers. I look around. I'm not sure this even qualifies as a restaurant. It's just an RV at the edge of the beach, behind the motel, with three beat-up picnic tables beside it. I take a tentative bite of the eggs, expecting to gag. But they're surprisingly good, and I'm starving.

"Here's the thing," Jas says finally. "Jet Skis cost money."

"Of course they do."

"Jet Skis," Jas repeats, "cost money. Plane tickets cost money. Surfboards cost money and foot straps cost money and even towropes cost money."

"I get it," I say. "You can't surf the world's biggest and best waves for free."

"Exactly," Jas agrees. He leans back, lacing his hands at the base of his head, straightening his legs out in front of him.

I have to move over so that our feet don't touch.

He shrugs again and sits back up, leaning toward me, his elbows on the table. "I was just trying to make us some money."

I look at my scrambled eggs. "But at what cost?"

"You sound just like Pete. 'It's not worth it'—that's what he'd tell me over and over again. I told him it was only temporary, just until I saved up enough to get us a Ski and some tickets. But Pete kicked me out before I made that much. Course," Jas adds, taking a sip of coffee, "I didn't go far. Pete may have hated me, but his wasn't the only empty house in Kensie."

"So he lives on one side of the beach and you live on the other."

"And he steals to put enough scraps together to feed the strays who show up at his house from time to time, and I sell drugs to make enough money to have running water and electricity and a Jet Ski and all the boards I want."

He smiles, but he doesn't sound pleased with himself. Quietly, he says, "If I hadn't been selling, Wendy, someone else would have." He's saying it to me, but he doesn't sound like he even believes it himself.

Shaking his head, he continues. "Pete and his crew still make it to the big waves sometimes. The local ones. But the ones across the globe? He just can't get there."

"Neither can you, apparently," I counter, and Jas's blue eyes fix on me. "I mean, you saved up all that money and bought yourself all those supplies, but you're still not out there, traveling the world, conquering those waves. Not like you planned anyway."

"No," Jas agrees, "not like I planned." He rests his forehead in his hands and takes a deep breath. "I did what I had to do," he says. His voice sounds muffled and far away. "I'm not going to lie—I would do it again." He looks up now, his eyes piercing and bright in the sunlight.

"Do you ever think of going back?" I ask, nodding my head in the direction of the mountains, in the direction of his childhood home. "You know, just to see your parents again, just for a second? To let them know that you're okay?"

Jas nods, breaking his gaze with me to look at the mountains above us. He presses his hands flat onto the table, just inches away from mine. I don't think he's going to answer me, but finally he looks at me with his clear blue eyes and says, "*Am* I okay?"

I don't mean to do it, but in a second I've taken his hand in mine, squeezing it tight. His flesh is cool, and the callus on his thumb rubs my knuckles softly, so softly, softer than I ever imagined anyone could or would touch me.

26

JAS IS HEAVING MY DUFFEL BAG INTO THE BACK of the truck when he turns to me. "I've got an idea," he says.

"What?" I answer, walking around to the passenger side of the car. He rushes to beat me there and hold the door open for me. My hair is still wet from my morning shower; drying in the ocean air, it even has the tiniest bit of a wave to it, instead of hanging stick-straight down my back like it usually does.

Jas climbs into the driver's seat. "There's a bar not too far from here. The Jolly Roger. I spent a lot of time there after I ran away. It's an old-school kinda place. Lots of surfers, lots of skin." He pauses, then adds, "Lots of substances."

"You think someone there might know my brothers?" I ask, cutting to the chase. Jas always hesitates before he mentions drugs and my brothers in the same sentence, like he hates to remind me about that part of them. It'd be kind of sweet, except for the fact that he's the person who sold them the drugs in the first place.

Jas nods. "But, Wendy, listen—" Jas's voice shifts, lowering an octave. "It's a bad scene."

I almost laugh; Pete used exactly the same words to describe Jas's side of Kensie, the first night I spent there. "Jas, no offense or anything, but I'm a big girl and you're a drug dealer. Won't we fit right in?"

He doesn't answer right away, just twists the keys in the ignition. I jump when the truck roars to life. "It's a long shot," he says, "but your brothers might've stopped there on their way up the coast months back. Someone might remember . . ."

"Supplying them?" I offer, and Jas nods. He pulls the car out of the lot.

"Well, then," I say, "I guess we're headed to the Jolly Roger."

. . . . .

Darkness falls earlier than usual; Jas explains that the storm is coming down from Canada, the one that's going to cause Witch Tree to break. He hands me his phone and shows me an image of a weather map, tracking the storm.

"Looks like the wave will break sometime tomorrow morning," he says, studying the map.

"Who knew surfers were such meteorology geeks?" I say, handing it back to him.

Jas laughs.

Even the parking lot of the Jolly Roger looks dangerous. First of all, it's not even paved; it's just a field of dirt next to a shack. The beach is right across the street, but it looks gritty somehow, the water not quite so blue, the sand gray with tar or dirt. Cars and motorcycles are parked haphazardly across the lot so that Jas has to squeeze his truck into a corner, the back half popping out onto the road behind us. A bare, grimy yellow lightbulb hangs above the door, flickering on and off.

"How do you even know this place is called the Jolly Roger?" I ask. "There's not exactly a sign over the door."

Jas smiles grimly. "You're just somebody who knows—or you aren't."

"Surfers," I say.

"Not just surfers."

I nod, unclicking my seat belt.

"You ready for this?" Jas asks.

I nod again, trying not to look nervous.

"You could stay in the car if you want to," Jas offers, but I shake my head. "That's what I thought," he says.

I take a deep breath. We've come this far, halfway across the state. What's a few steps farther?

I'm shaking as I follow him across the parking lot, and it takes me a second to realize that it's not fear, but excitement. For all I know, John and Michael are inside the Jolly Roger right now, just a few yards away, on the other side of a beat-up door that I notice, when Jas opens it, is halfway off its hinges. They could be in there just killing time before Witch Tree breaks in the morning. Jas might walk right up to them and tell them to follow him out to the parking lot. They wouldn't hesitate. They'd assume that Jas was about to hook them up. Imagine their surprise when they see me standing beside him.

It's sad how relieved I am that they'd follow a drug dealer wherever he led them, like Jas is some kind of pied piper. They'll be so disappointed when Jas doesn't actually have anything to sell them, more disappointed still when we get home and it's them going off to rehab. Because they're the ones who need help, not me.

Inside, it's so dimly lit that my eyes have to adjust to the darkness, even though it wasn't exactly bright outside either. Sitting at the bar are about a half dozen men and teenage boys, nursing beers or cocktails, one or two looking so skinny that, despite their muscles and their tans, they seem sick. A few splintered tables dot the room, most of them empty.

"Wendy," Jas whispers, tugging my arm; I look down, surprised to see that he's holding my hand, not exactly sure when that happened. "I'm going to go into the back room."

"What's in there?"

Jas shakes his head. "Just wait for me out here."

A woman staggers across the room and practically falls into a chair beside a table and promptly passes out. Other than her, I'm the only female here.

"Okay," I say, reaching into my purse for my phone and scrolling through the photos. "Here's their picture. There's, like, twelve of them on there, but this one is the most recent. Their names are John and Michael and they're twins, but not identical. And they're about five feet eight, or that's what they were the last time I saw them. Michael is maybe a half an inch taller and he never lets John forget it, even though technically John is older. He was born ninety seconds ahead of Michael. And—"

"Wendy," Jas says gently, "I know them, remember?"

I nod. He squeezes my hand once more before he leaves. "Be careful," he says.

"You, too."

He slips me the car keys before he leaves. "Go back to the car if you need to," he says.

By the time Jas has disappeared behind an unmarked swinging door, I'm wondering if I should run back to the car right away. Pete would have wanted me to *stay* in the car to begin with.

I shake my head and remind myself that I'm supposed to be the one searching for my brothers. Even with Jas in the back room, I can be asking around. At the very least, it will keep me too busy to be scared.

I walk straight to the bar and order myself a beer. I get the feeling this isn't the kind of place where they're going to ask me for ID.

Someone lights a cigarette beside me. I turn and come face-to-face with the scariest-looking man I've ever seen. He's not as tall as Jas, but muscles bulge from beneath his wife-beater, like he spends his days lifting weights on the beach. He's grinning at me; one of his bottom teeth is missing.

I consider mentioning that it's illegal to smoke in a bar in California, but instead I ask if I can bum one of his cigarettes. When he leans in to light it for me, I wonder if he can tell that I've never actually smoked a cigarette before.

"Thanks," I say, swallowing a cough.

"No problem," he replies, and winks.

"So," I say, taking a drag on the cigarette, "come here often?" I exhale, watching the smoke rise in plumes around his face.

"Aw, come on, beautiful, you're not going to use that line, are you?"

He leans in so close that when he speaks I can taste his breath: cigarettes and liquor, yesterday's lunch and last night's vomit. I resist the urge to back away.

"You're a little honey, ain'tcha? So pretty and clean."

I shake my head. There are no clues to be found with him. I slide down from my seat, cigarette in one hand, beer in the other.

"Nice meeting you," I say awkwardly as I turn to walk away, looking around for someone else to ask, hopefully someone slightly less terrifying.

But he gets up and follows me across the room. "We didn't exactly meet, did we? And I'd sure like the chance to get to know you better."

I grimace, tossing my cigarette onto the sawdust-covered floor.

"I came here with someone," I say carefully.

"Just 'cause you came here with someone doesn't mean you're leaving with him," he says, grinning again and displaying his missing tooth. I wonder how he lost it.

The woman who passed out a few minutes ago is moaning as she lifts her head off the table. I consider sitting down and offering her my beer as a pretext for asking her some questions. But the man beside me is licking his lips; his breath sounds like he's practically panting. So I head for the door, gripping Jas's keys so tightly it hurts. I may want to ask more questions, but I need to get away from this creep even more.

Soon I'm sprinting across the lot, dropping my beer on the ground, and climbing into the driver's seat of Jas's truck, checking to make sure that the doors are locked, the windows rolled up.

Finally safe, I exhale, the taste of cigarette smoke heavy in my mouth.

A knock on the passenger side window startles me and I jump. I don't know why I didn't think he'd follow me into the parking lot.

"Open up," he says softly. "I won't bite." I shake my head. He knocks again, so hard this time that the entire truck rattles. I'm pretty sure he could tear the door off with his bare hands.

I reach into my purse. But then I remember that I can't call anyone for help. Jas has my cell phone. My hands are shaking so hard that I can't even fit the keys into the ignition.

Shit. *Shit*. I press the horn, barely tapping it, but the sound is enough to make the guy drop his hand. He grins and steps away, crouching down. When he stands up, he's holding a rock, lifting his arm behind him like a pitcher winding up for the throw. A heartbeat after he releases the rock, the side view mirror on the passenger side shatters into a thousand pieces.

Now I lean on the horn like my life depends on it. Maybe it does.

Jas comes running out of the bar, charging right at the guy. They fall to the ground; I can't see them from where I'm sitting. Instead, I just see dirt flying up from the ground below.

Suddenly, Jas springs up and runs around to the driver's side. I unlock the door.

"Move, Wendy!" he shouts. "Move!"

I nod, scrambling into the passenger seat and handing Jas the keys. He shoves them into the ignition and we speed off so fast that I don't even get a chance to look back, to see in what condition Jas left the other man lying on the ground.

"Are you okay?" Jas asks. I open my mouth to say yes, but I can't get the words out. I lift my hands to my face, surprised to find that there are tears running down my cheeks. I brush them away and take a deep breath, but I can't take a deep breath because I can't stop shaking.

"Wendy," Jas says, his voice so deep that it cuts through my shaking. "Wendy, look at me." He takes his eyes off the road just long enough to look into my eyes. "You're okay. He didn't hurt you. I would never have let him get to you."

He lifts his foot off the gas slightly; we're back on the highway now, and he slows us down until we're a little bit closer to the speed limit.

"I would never have let him get to you," Jas repeats.

I nod. I believe him.

27

"WELL, YOU WERE RIGHT," I SAY AFTER A FEW MORE miles of silence. My pulse has slowed to an almost normal beat, and the tissues I pulled from my purse have wiped away all traces of my tears. "The Jolly Roger is a bad scene."

Jas laughs. "Told ya so," he says, and I smile. "Hey," he says gently, "I've got some news. There was a guy in the back who recognized Michael and John."

"Really?" I ask, my heartbeat quickening again. "Oh my god, should we go back?"

"Back there?" Jas laughs. "Your friend's probably still waiting for us in the parking lot. If he regained consciousness."

"But if someone there knew John and Michael—"

Jas shakes his head. "This guy had shared a motel room with your brothers a while back—sometime this winter."

"Sometime after Pete kicked them out," I say.

"Don't be so hard on Pete," Jas says. "*I* was the reason he had to kick them out."

I look over at him, shocked that he's taking the blame. That's when I see that Jas's right hand is bleeding all over the steering wheel.

"Your hand!"

Jas shrugs. "There was glass on the ground." Whether it was from the shattered mirror or just from the dozens of broken beer bottles littered across the Jolly Roger's parking lot, I don't know.

"We've got to get it cleaned up."

"Believe me," Jas says, "I've had a lot worse."

I don't want to imagine just what that means. I see a sign for a service area coming up and I say, "Pull over there."

Jas keeps going straight.

"Now!" I say firmly, and this time, to my surprise, he listens. The fog is thick as we curl along the exit ramp.

"Now it's my turn to tell you to stay in the car," I say, hopping down from my seat. I run into the shop next to the gas station. When I come back, carrying water, bandages, and a cup of ice, Jas is sitting on the tailgate of the truck, his long legs hanging down and swinging back and forth like a little kid's.

"I thought I told you to stay in the car," I scold. I hop onto the truck beside him and pull a towel out from between a couple of the surfboards, pouring the ice into it. In addition to his bleeding hand, an ugly bruise is blossoming above his left cheekbone. I press the ice to his face, and he leans into my touch before placing his hand over my own.

"I'm sorry," I say, dropping my hand and opening up a package of gauze. I pull his other hand into my lap, cleaning out his cut as gingerly as possible.

"What for? You didn't punch me."

"We went to that place because of me," I say. "And for what? Another dead end. We don't really know any more than we did before."

"It was my idea," Jas says, cringing as I clean the gravel from his wound. The cut is long and skinny, horizontal across his palm. I can tell now that it's not deep, at least.

"Will you be able to surf tomorrow?"

"Takes more than a few bumps and bruises to keep me out of the water."

I smile, nodding.

The fog turns into a light drizzle, soaking our clothes and the truck beneath us. I shiver, but I don't want to move.

"We're not far from Witch Tree now," he says. "Surfers from all over the place will be there tomorrow. No one's going to want to miss this swell."

"So if my brothers are still out there, they won't want to miss it, either."

Jas shakes his head, dropping the ice into the truck behind him. "Wendy," he says, "I didn't mean—"

"I know," I say, but a lump is rising slowly in my throat. My tongue feels like it's made of cement. Jas's cut is clean now and the bleeding has almost stopped; I cover his hand with Band-Aids, spread across his palm. When I'm done, Jas lifts his un-damaged left hand to my face. I close my eyes and imagine the way these hands propel him through the water when he paddles into the surf.

"They could be there," he says. He sounds so sure, so certain. I open my eyes; his face is just inches from mine. His blue eyes are clearer than water. His breath is cool on my skin. He begins to move his hand from my face, but I cover it with my own hand, pressing his touch even closer. His fingers are warm and solid, as strong as the rest of him.

Before he can back away, I lean forward and kiss him. Softly at first, like it's my first kiss and I don't quite understand the mechanics of it. For a split second, he doesn't kiss me back, and I think maybe he's not going to. Just the thought makes my stomach hurt, makes me want him more, makes me want to lean in closer, press my lips to his that much harder. And just when I think I can't take it anymore, he kisses me back.

He lifts his wounded hand from my lap so that his palms are on either side of my face, cupping my cheeks. The Band-Aids are rough against my skin; I can smell his blood and his sweat, the stale beer that must have soaked into his clothes in the bar's parking lot. I weave my fingers through his dark hair, gently brushing out tiny pieces of gravel from the ground.

The kiss seems to last forever and yet seems to end too soon. Jas is the one who finally pulls away.

"We should get going," he says, jumping down to the ground. He has a look on his face, in the fog and the rain and the cloudy light shining down from the streetlamps above us, that I've seen before. A look I now understand is reserved just for me.

"Hey," I say, emboldened, "that day, on the beach at Kensington. You didn't really come to Pete's side of the beach for the waves, did you? You were there because of me, weren't you?"

Jas smiles. "What do you think?" he says. He lifts me down from the truck and takes my hand in his, leading me back to the passenger side, opening the door for me. When he gets in on the other side, I slide across the seat to lean against him and rest my head on his shoulder. As he pulls back onto the freeway, he puts his arm around me and I fall asleep listening to the patter of the rain on the roof of the truck.

· · · · ·

I wake up a couple hours later in another motel parking lot, almost identical to the one we left behind this morning. The only difference is that this parking lot is filled and the sign flashing VACANCY has the word NO in front of it.

The rain has increased from a drizzle to a pour, and Jas runs from the motel lobby to the car.

"Come on out," he says, opening my door. He takes off his sweatshirt and holds it over my head to keep me dry, the other arm around me, holding me close. He's so warm that I wonder what it would be like to crawl up inside him.

"It says no vacancy," I say, pointing to the sign above us.

Jas shakes his head. "Honey, I made these reservations days ago. The very second I heard about that swell."

I stand on my tiptoes and kiss him again, quickly this time.

When I pull away, he says, "I got us separate beds again."

"You didn't have to do that," I reply, winding my arms around his waist as we walk toward our room. I mean it. I want to stay this close to him for as long as I possibly can.

28

JAS'S LONG BODY CURLS AROUND ME WHEN WE finally fall asleep. I concentrate on the weight of his upper arm resting on my rib cage, the heat of his knees pressing into my calves. I press my back against his front, feeling the muscles of his chest flex as he tightens his hold on me.

Soon, Jas's breathing grows slower and his muscles relax. He's asleep, and I'm wide awake. Even though I hate to put any space between us, I roll away. He needs his rest for tomorrow; I don't want to keep him awake just because I can't sleep.

And I'm not sure I want to talk to him about my reasons for being restless. How did I get here, lying in bed with a guy whose last name I don't even know? I don't even know the name of the town this motel is in. He's a drug dealer, he can be violent, he can be cruel. He's the reason Pete kicked my brothers out in January, the reason I'm still no closer to finding them than I was the day I graduated high school.

And yet, listening to the waves crashing through the open

window, I know that I *am* closer. I sit up and slide off the bed. We chose the bed closest to the window; Jas threw my duffel bag on the second bed, but otherwise, it's completely undisturbed.

I've never done anything like this. My god, until last night, I'd never even been in a motel like this. There's only one lamp in the room, on a nightstand in between the two beds, and when Jas tried to turn it on earlier, the bulb flickered weakly. I don't even want to think about the last time they cleaned the bathroom; there's a ring of sand around the drain. And every surface in the room is covered in dust, as though no one has stayed here for months. Which, I guess, they haven't. This place probably only fills up when the nearby waves break, and according to Jas, that hasn't happened since January.

When my brothers were here. Maybe they stayed in this very motel. It would have been too cold to camp out on the beach. Maybe they convinced some friends to let them crash on the floor of their room, or maybe they used up the last of their allowance money to pay for a room of their own. No; they would have long since spent whatever money they'd taken when they left home.

I glance back at Jas; he's rolled onto his back now and is snoring softly. The sound is comforting, a reminder that I'm not alone. With his drug money, he could afford to stay anywhere. He could have booked us into the nearest five-star hotel. The fact that he chose this place makes me like him even more. This is where the surfers stay. There's nowhere we could have stayed that would have been closer to the water.

I grab his sweatshirt and slip it on, breathing in the smell of him: soap and sweat, beer and salt, and something else, something uniquely Jas. I slip out the door, careful to close it as quietly as possible behind me. I don't want him to follow me.

The rain has stopped, but the air is clouded with mist. I can barely see three feet in front of me. I walk barefoot across the motel parking lot and onto the beach, feeling the sand between my toes. It's cold beneath my feet, no trace of the day's heat left behind.

The roar of the ocean grows louder and louder, not just because I'm getting closer to the water but because the waves are picking up. Witch Tree might not be breaking until tomorrow morning, but the ocean is getting ready for it now, like a dancer warming up before her big show. The moon is full above me, pulling the tides every which way.

I walk until the sand goes from moist to wet beneath my feet, until I can feel the waves lapping my toes. I hear something to my left—a shout, a laugh, a cry, I'm not sure. In the distance, where there was only darkness before, I see a hint of light, someone sparking a fire. I watch as it grows from a single flame to a roaring bonfire, glowing and brilliant through the fog.

I smile, remembering the bonfire on the beach the night that I graduated, the first time I saw Pete. I'd never seen anyone move on the water the way he did; he looked like it was what he was made to do. Was it luck that made Pete leave Kensington that night, head down to Newport, to the beach where my classmates and I were celebrating?

Even though I'm yards away from the bonfire on the beach now, I feel warmer just knowing that it's there. I was falling hard for Pete, and now I'm falling fast for Jas. How is that possible? To feel such intense emotions for two different people, one right after the other? Maybe Fiona and my parents were right, after all. Maybe I am crazy. At least a little bit. I'd have to be a little bit crazy to do the things I've done over the past few months, wouldn't I?

And I'd have to be at least a little bit crazy to have enjoyed it all as much as I have. Even despite the fear and the heartache, despite Pete's lies and Jas's dust, I've never felt so alive.

Another sound floats down the beach from the bonfire. A shout this time. Someone calling someone else's name. Must be a group of surfers, getting ready for tomorrow. Maybe they're celebrating the waves to come. I squint in the fog, trying to make out shapes of people sitting around the fire; from here, all I can see are shadows.

But then one of the shadows turns; I see a profile, one that I recognize. I break into a run, but the fire is farther away than I realized. I'm panting by the time another silhouette comes into view.

Between heaving breaths, I shout, "John! Michael!" I expect them to turn when they hear my voice.

"John! Michael!" I scream hoarsely. I cough; I'm getting a stitch in my right side. I wish I were stronger, faster, fitter. Jas or Pete would be there by now. They'd have sprinted down the beach in two seconds flat.

"Please!" I shout, and as I do, the figures scatter. The wind whips off the ocean, and the fire climbs to a terrifying height; for a second, it looks like it's about to explode, and I freeze in midstep. Just as suddenly, the flames begin to dwindle until it looks like they're going to fade away entirely.

"No!" I shout, willing myself to run faster, breathe harder, anything to get there before my brothers have the chance to disappear again. "Please!" I say once more, but by the time I'm close enough to smell the smoke from what's now a dying fire, everyone has gone. The wind blows my hair into my face, blinding me. I tear it away, wishing I could rip it off. I turn in circles, calling my brothers' names, but the wind carries my voice away before the words get very far.

I'm sweating beneath Jas's shirt, but I've never been so cold. Even the tears streaming down my cheeks feel like ice. I am so sick and tired of chasing phantoms. I just want to find my brothers and hold on to them, feel their flesh beneath my grip, tactile and undeniable.

Slowly, regaining my breath, I walk back the way I came. The dim lights from the motel lobby are barely visible from here, but they're enough to guide my way back. I look up at the sky as I walk, waiting for a break in the clouds.

I make a wish on the second star I see.

29

AT FOUR A.M., JAS SHAKES ME GENTLY AWAKE. MY
clothes are still damp from my midnight run through the fog,
but if Jas notices, he doesn't say anything.

"It's time to go," he says, kissing my shoulder. "The witch is
calling our name."

A burst of adrenaline makes me bounce from the bed. The
wave is breaking.

On the way to the harbor, the fog is so thick that Jas drives at
a snail's pace, careful around the curves in the road. I can't see
six feet in front of us—are people really going to surf in this
soup? Jas explains that we're heading to the harbor to rent a boat
for the day.

"Why do we need a boat?"

"Witch Tree doesn't break onshore; you have to take a boat to
get there."

"How can a wave break in the middle of the ocean?"

"Waves break over changes on the ocean floor. Reefs, that

kind of thing. There's a wave down near San Diego called Cortes that breaks over a sunken island.

"I'll need to find a partner to tow me in," he continues. Jas already explained that the only way to surf a wave like Witch Tree is to tow into it on a Jet Ski like the one in the back of the truck. "But I'm pretty sure that finding a partner won't be a problem once we get to the harbor and offer someone a free ride out."

I nod, wondering how much it costs to rent a boat and a captain for the day, wondering how much a Jet Ski costs.

"That's an ugly-looking mess you've got on your face," I say. His bruise has morphed from purple to yellow overnight.

Jas laughs, wincing. "If I get my face rearranged like this too many times, you won't want me anymore, huh?"

"You were too handsome before," I answer. "Now you look a little bit more like the rest of us."

Jas laughs again, resting his right hand on my knee. His palm is still covered in Band-Aids. The cut will sting when the salt water seeps in below the bandages, but I know he doesn't care. Like he said, it takes more than a few bumps and bruises to keep him out of the water.

I almost tell him what I saw on the beach last night; I want to talk about the bonfire and seeing John and Michael. I should be more excited: I saw them, they're here, Jas was right. Surely they will be at the harbor today, hoping for a ride out to Witch Tree. But I keep my mouth shut. I'm not really sure I saw anything at all last night. Maybe it was someone else. Maybe it was just a waking dream. I press the heels of my hands into my eyes, like maybe if I just rub them hard enough, I'll be able to distinguish dream from reality, know phantom from human.

"Okay?" Jas says, glancing over at me as he pulls the truck into a crowded sandy parking lot near the docks. Even tethered to land, the boats are rocking and rolling, noisily bumping into the pier. I've never seen an ocean so choppy; it looks like a ski slope covered in moguls.

"Fine," I answer, unclicking my seat belt. But my hands are shaking.

Before he opens the door, Jas leans over, pressing his bruised cheek against my smooth one, steadying me.

It's cold on the pier; the sun is hours from rising, and judging from the cloud cover I'm not sure it's going to make an appearance at all today. The wind whips my hair into my face, and I struggle to pull it back into a ponytail. Despite the hour, the place is packed; half the crowd already have their wet suits on, their surfboards propped up beside them. A camera crew is struggling with their equipment, hoping for a shot of the best ride of the day. The air feels charged with the power of the summer storm, the swell that simply should not be coming this time of year. Jas told me that the storms usually show up a few days behind the big waves, but I don't think this storm cares about how it's usually done. I wonder how far all these surfers traveled. Like Jas said, surfing these waves in August is a once-in-a-lifetime experience. Not that it feels like the beginning of August. It's freezing.

As Jas heads for the boats, I weave my way through the crowd, looking for John and Michael. I concentrate on listening for the sounds of their voices above the howling wind, the waves, the chatter of the people who've gathered. No one seems to mind my bumping into them—they're all focused on the water—but still, I wish I were tiny like Belle. She'd be able to squeeze between these people easily, like a mouse disappearing into its hole.

Suddenly, a deafening shout on a megaphone: "The harbor is closed. I repeat, no boats will be launching from the harbor today."

He tries to explain that conditions are so bad and visibility so limited that the Coast Guard has shut down the beaches for miles around, but it's nearly impossible to hear him as the crowd erupts into a series of shouts. I'm jostled about as the surfers raise their arms and their enormous boards in protest. No one will be surfing Witch Tree today after all.

The crowd disperses fast as everyone scrambles to make their way to the next wave.

"Wait!" I beg, shouting my brothers' names. But my voice is carried off by the wind.

I hear someone say they're heading up the coast to Maverick's, someone else say they're gonna head down to Killers, a wave in Mexico; the swell is sure to generate heavy waves down south in a couple days, too. And it's easier to get around the Coast Guard down there.

"Wait!" I shout again, chasing the surfers into the parking lot.

I feel the heat of Jas's hand slipping into mine. "Come on," he says, nodding in the direction of his truck. "Let's head back to the motel."

I shake my head. "Where do we go next?" I ask desperately, but I let him lead me to the car. How could such a large crowd disappear so quickly? I look frantically at the few surfers who are left, trying to pick out a familiar face.

And then I see one. Not a face I've been looking for, but the last face I expected to see.

"Pete," I say softly. Somehow, over the wind and the waves, he hears me. My belly twists inside of me; I drop Jas's hand and stop walking. Jas pauses and turns, sees just who I'm staring at.

I rub my hands against each other as though I'm trying to keep warm, but the truth is, I'm trying to rub Jas's touch away. Why don't I want Pete to see me holding Jas's hand? The last time I saw him, I told him I didn't ever want to see him again. So why do I care whether he knows that I'm with Jas—*am* I with Jas?

Belle appears from behind Pete, scowling first at me and then at Jas. She doesn't seem surprised to see us here. Pete, on the other hand, looks completely floored. I feel myself blushing hotly.

"What are you doing?" Pete shouts. His words are directed at me, but he's looking at Jas.

"I'm looking for John and Michael," I shout back, but my voice sounds thin, reedy, weak. Pete crosses the parking lot until he's so close I could reach out and touch him. Belle follows, along with a few faces I recognize, including Hughie and Matt.

"I'm looking for my brothers," I repeat. Even though it's the truth, it feels like a lie.

Pete takes a step closer—not to me, but to Jas.

"Don't use her to get back at me," he says icily.

The wind picks up, sweeping sand into my eyes, blinding me. "What?" I shout.

I hear Jas's voice saying, "I'm not—" but then Pete cuts him off.

"Not that I should be surprised," he says. "It's just your style. And you never could get over it that Belle chose me."

I try to open my eyes, but my body won't cooperate. The sand is making tears leak from beneath my eyelids.

"Once she sobered up, though, the choice was obvious. Tell me, Jas, did you have to drug Wendy to get her, too?"

I shake my head. In my mind's eye, I can see Jas's face last night when he leaned in to kiss me. The long muscles in his torso when he lifted his shirt over his head. The arch of his back when he reached for the light switch, plunging the room into darkness. His hands on my skin; his face next to mine.

"Pete," I say, forcing my eyes open. His face is blurry in front of me, an impressionist painting. "What are you talking about?"

"Didn't he tell you, Wendy? Belle used to be Jas's *favorite* duster." He says the word *favorite* like it's something dirty. "Until she wised up and left him. I gave her a place to stay after he bled her dry. And he never forgave me for it."

"I don't understand," I say.

"Oh my god, Wendy, isn't it obvious?" Belle shouts. "I was with Jas until Pete rescued me, got me sober, taught me to surf. And now Jas is using you to get back at Pete." She turns from me to Jas. "An eye for an eye, right, sweetheart?"

Finally, Jas speaks. "It's not like that, Wendy," he says softly. "Not at all."

Pete is standing so close to him that he can't even turn to face me.

"Really?" Pete says. "Tell me how it is, then. When will it be enough? Do you have to mess with everyone I care about?"

I take a step back, away from them both. Nothing that they're saying makes any sense, and yet everything they're saying is perfectly clear. My tears have washed the sand from my eyes and

I'm able to see clearly when Pete lifts his fist and brings it crashing down on Jas's face, right above the bruise that's already there. I hear Jas shout in pain and watch him try to shove Pete away; he doesn't throw a single punch, just holds his hands up to protect himself. He's inches taller than Pete, but he looks completely defenseless.

I turn from the fight and break into a run until there's too much fog between us for me to see any trace of them at all.

30

I RUN ONTO A PATH AT THE EDGE OF THE PARKING lot, up onto the rocks that overlook the ocean. On prettier days, this is probably a place where parents take their kids to play, where young couples bring their dogs for a hike, maybe where first dates go for a romantic view of the water. But there's nothing romantic about the ocean today, about the waves crashing angrily against the rocks. The spray is high enough to reach me, soaking my ponytail, drenching my skin. I shiver.

I'd almost forgotten that *this* is the reason everyone else came here—for these waves. The waves brought Pete and Belle here. They didn't come here looking for me, or for John and Michael; they came to surf. Maybe that's all Jas wanted to do, too. Maybe I was just a pleasant enough companion to take along for the ride. Or maybe he was using me to get back at Pete for taking Belle from him, just like Pete said.

But then why did he suggest going to the bar yesterday? Why did he put himself in danger just to ask about my brothers? I sit down, even though the rocks are sharp and cold beneath me, and rest my head in my hands.

Even if I head up to Maverick's or down to Killers, continuing my search for my brothers alone, I'll still be chasing just a rumor, a whisper, a hope. I haven't found clues, just dead ends. A hopeless detective on an endless scavenger hunt.

The heat of someone's body beside me makes me look up.

Pete.

"Hey," he says, sitting down next to me.

"I'm surprised you're willing to sit next to me," I say. "You know, after I joined forces with your arch nemesis and all."

Pete laughs at my choice of words, as though he and Jas are two superheroes battling it out for world domination.

"It's my fault you're with him, Wendy. If I'd just been honest with you from the start—"

"Why weren't you?" I interrupt. "Really. I'm not angry anymore."

"You're not?"

I shake my head. I'm too tired to be angry. "I just want to understand it."

"I told you," Pete says. "I wanted more time with you." He looks so earnest, so sweet, like a little kid who's begging his mother for another slice of cake, another piece of candy, more time at the playground, just a few more minutes on the beach.

"You thought that if I knew you couldn't help me find my brothers, I'd immediately lose all interest in you?" I ask.

If only he knew. The truth is, I was drawn to him from the very first time I saw him on the beach, though it seems like a million years ago now. When I followed him into Kensington the next day, it was because I was looking for my brothers, sure, but I also followed him just because I wanted to. Because I wanted to find out where he was headed.

"No," he answers. "But I felt awful once I knew they were your brothers and they were missing. And I felt responsible. I knew if you knew I'd kicked them out, you'd never forgive me."

He doesn't look at me when he says it, but at the rough sea. I follow his gaze. What does it feel like to be ready and willing to take on an ocean like this only to be told that you're not allowed to leave dry land? All those surfers at the harbor today—what will they do with all that pent-up energy now that the Coast Guard has shut the beach down? It's strange to think of the ocean as something that can be closed for business, locked up and gated and guarded. Is there really any place to put all that momentum when your chance has been taken away from you, all because the thing you want is simply too dangerous to attempt?

Returning my gaze to Pete, I shrug. "Isn't that what you're supposed to do with addicts? Kick them out? Tough love or something?" I guess that's what my parents were trying to do when they tried to ship me to Montana.

My poor parents. They must be worried sick. I picture them at home in the glass house, walking around silently, wondering what they did so wrong, how they failed so spectacularly as parents that all three of their children felt the need to flee. And Nana; my dog probably misses me most of all. Suddenly, I miss her so much my stomach hurts. My parents, too. They were just trying to help me.

Pete shakes his head. "I didn't kick them out for their own good, Wendy." He pauses, taking a deep breath. "I kicked them out for *my* own good. For Belle's. For Hughie's. I kicked them out because I hate Jas and I didn't want anyone in my house who was involved with him."

Pete looks at me now, his hazel eyes fiery even in the mist.

"I should have let them stay. I should have *begged* them to stay. I should have helped them get sober, the same way I did for Belle."

"You helped Belle because you love her," I say.

"But I should have helped her because it was the *right* thing to do. I should have helped your brothers because it was the right thing to do."

His voice is thick with guilt. He stops talking suddenly. An enormous wave crashes against the rocks, sending up spray and soaking us, but neither of us moves.

"I really thought that I'd find them here," I say finally. "That is really why I'm here, you know. And now, who knows where they're headed?" I'm surprised that I'm able to get the words out around the lump in my throat. When the tears finally overflow from beneath my eyelids, Pete stands and pulls me into his arms.

"Wendy," he says, and my name sounds different somehow. Important. In Pete's arms, I feel safe and warm. Like nothing bad can happen to me, not as long as I let him hold me.

"I know you miss your brothers," he says. "And I'm so, so sorry for the part I played. I'm sorry that I made them leave, and I'm sorry for lying to you."

I nod, my cheek damp against his shirt. He must be freezing, here in the wind and the damp in nothing but a T-shirt and board shorts, but somehow, being in his arms still makes me feel warm.

"I know that you'll see them again, Wendy, one way or another. They're out there." He gestures to the ocean. "They're surfing somewhere. I know that."

I nod. Could Pete be right? Maybe John and Michael are destined to spend their lives searching for their next great ride, just like Pete, and maybe just like Jas, too. Maybe I should try to learn to live with that. I *need* to learn to live with it if I'm going to have any kind of life of my own.

"Wendy," Pete says gently, "do you think you can be happy, even with them gone?"

"I don't know," I answer honestly.

"I do," Pete says firmly. "You were happy in Kensington. With me. Weren't you?"

I close my eyes. I remember taking a wave while the boys cheered me on from the beach, standing in front of a bonfire to keep warm, sitting on the cliffs with Pete holding me the way he is now. I was never just there to search for my brothers; I spent my days and nights in that house on the cliffs and on the beach below falling for Pete. I never felt so free, never felt so alive. Jas said living in Kensington agreed with me, and he wasn't wrong. Maybe Pete knew that all along.

"Yes," I say finally. "I was happy there."

"Then come back with me," Pete says quickly. "Come home."

My eyes still closed, I see myself walking into Jas's house; the heat and the rhythm of his party, the warmth of the carpet on his floor. I see his blue eyes spotting me from across the room, beckoning me closer. I feel the heat of his body against mine, smell the warm scent of his skin. I don't belong in that drug-saturated house with Jas, but I don't think I belong in the abandoned house with Pete, Belle, and the boys, either.

Still, Pete is right. It's time for me to go home.

"I can't," I say softly, disentangling myself from his hold. The wind rushes off the water, blowing my clothes flat against my body until it feels like I could take flight. "I'm sorry."

I turn away from his hazel eyes and his warm arms, begin walking back down to the road. Somehow, I'm going to make my way back to Newport, to the glass house on the hill, to my parents and my dog, to the life I left behind. The life that's waiting for me. But as I walk away, I hear Pete's voice carrying over the wind.

"Belle and the boys and I are going to stick around here for a few days," he says. "So, if you change your mind, Wendy, I'll be waiting."

31

MY DUFFEL BAG FEELS HEAVY WHEN I LIFT IT OFF the second bed in the motel room. It's hard to believe that I was so happy here in Jas's arms just a few hours ago. The guy at reception told me that there's a bus stop about a mile down the road where I can catch a ride down the coast for only forty dollars. When that bus leaves, I intend to be on it. Once I'm closer to home, I'll call Fiona. Call my parents. I'll go to therapy if they want me to; I'll go to rehab. I'll do whatever they say I have to in order to be back home, to get my life back on track, to go to Stanford like I've been planning to do my whole life. I am *done* chasing phantoms.

"Don't leave," says a deep voice behind me, and I spin around, startled. I didn't hear Jas come in. Or has he been here the whole time?

"I'm going home," I say, shaking my head and walking toward the door. Jas blocks my way. "Please don't," I say softly. "I just want to go."

"Let me explain—" he starts, but I cut him off.

"I don't care if you only brought me here to get back at Pete and Belle. Maybe I should, but I really don't." Still too tired to be angry, I repeat, "I just want to go home."

"I can drive you."

"No thanks," I say, but he's still blocking my path. I could squeeze past him, push him out of my way, but the truth is, I don't want to be that close to him. I don't want to smell him and feel the heat of his skin next to mine.

"I didn't bring you here to get back at Pete," Jas says quietly. He steps aside, but much to my surprise, I don't run for the door.

Instead I ask, "Then why?"

"That day when you showed up in Kensington, that day when we first met—"

"Technically we didn't meet," I interrupt. "It's not like you said, 'Hi, I'm Jas, the local drug kingpin, nice to meet you.'"

He nods. "I know," he agrees. "It felt good. For once, there was someone pulling into my driveway who wasn't looking for dust. Someone who had no idea that mine was the house where you could always score."

I lower my duffel bag to the floor and sit on the edge of the bed. Jas continues.

"And watching you surf all those mornings on your own. You were fearless."

I shake my head. I didn't feel fearless. I was scared, but I just wanted to take those waves so much. Just like I wanted to find my brothers so much, more than anything. That desire was bigger than my fear—of going to Jas's party and taking dust, of climbing out my window and driving up the coast with a dangerous stranger, of going to the Jolly Roger.

Jas continues, "And when you showed up at my party, knowing who I was and what I did—I just wanted it to feel the way it felt when you came the first time, when you thought I was just some surfer living by the beach. Because that's all I ever wanted to be. And you were so angry at me, my god, I didn't know that someone on dust could be so angry."

"I don't really remember," I say, shrugging.

"Well, I do," Jas says. "I was stone-cold sober that night and I remember every word you said. You hated me then. It felt like a punch to the gut."

"So you showed up at my house when you heard Witch Tree was breaking to try to be my knight in shining armor?"

Jas shakes his head. "No," he says. "More like the other way around. I thought, if I could help this girl find her brothers, that would be the first step."

"The first step in what?"

"The first step in moving on, leaving my old life behind. See, Wendy, I started selling drugs to make enough money to buy a Jet Ski, a plane ticket, new surfboards and wax. When I started out, I saved every penny. I thought I would just deal for a few months and then move on with my life. But the truth is, I made enough money and more a long time ago. But I didn't stop dealing."

"Why?"

He shakes his head. "Maybe I forgot what I actually wanted to do with my life. I'm not sure."

"Yes, you are."

Jas takes a deep breath and says sadly, "Pete wouldn't come with me, not anymore."

I don't say anything, so he continues. "Wendy, I meant it when I said that I wanted to help you find your brothers. I have the money. We just have to follow the waves. Every time and everywhere a swell is predicted, we'll be there. Every time, until we find John and Michael. Wendy," he says, taking a step toward me, crouching down on the floor in front of me and taking my hand in his. "I don't just want to help you. I want to *be* with you. I want to start this new part of my life with you. Will you come with me?"

His blue eyes are filled with hope; he really believes that finding my brothers is his first step in leaving his old life behind, and I can see how badly he wants it. For a second, I allow myself to want it, too. It *could* be magical, picking up and heading off to Hawaii, Tahiti, Portugal, Mexico; tracking waves like bloodhounds, letting the weather determine our path. Letting Jas take the lead and hold my hand and carry my bags and open every door for me wherever we go.

But how far will we travel? How many days will there be like today? How many dead ends will it take until my heart breaks into so many pieces that nothing—not even Jas, strong as he is— can put it back together again?

I shake my head. Pete wants me with him in Kensington, wants to build a life with me in the house on the cliffs. Jas wants me for just the opposite reason—he wants to leave Kensington behind with me by his side.

Suddenly, I realize why Pete didn't tell me the truth about my brothers. Not just because he thought I'd hate him for kicking them out, but because he wanted to protect me from knowing that my brothers were addicts. From the very first day in Kensington, when he told me to let him take the lead, to let my worries go, he wanted to give me the things he thought would make me happy.

But Jas believes I'm strong enough to dive into the deep end with him. He wants to share his adventures with me; wants us to take on the world together. Together, he wants to find my brothers, no matter how sick or drug-addled they might be when we do.

I'm not sure I'm as strong as Jas thinks I am, as fearless. "I have to go home," I say finally. "I can't keep coming up against dead ends. I don't think I'll survive too many more of them."

I stand and lift my bag, and this time, Jas doesn't try to keep me from leaving. I keep my gaze focused on the ground; I don't want to see him staring at me when I walk away.

• • • • •

The bus stop isn't crowded. In fact, it's completely empty. It's not even really a bus stop at all so much as a beat-up, weather-stripped bench on the side of the road. But this is where the kid at the motel told me to go. He said the bus's schedule can be erratic, but it's sure to be here sometime today. All I have to do is wait.

I drop my bag and practically fall onto the bench. It's not even seven in the morning; at home, Fiona and my parents are just beginning their days. Strange, because this already feels like the longest day of my life, and I still have such a long way to go.

I zip up my sweatshirt and pull the hood over my head. It's a Stanford sweatshirt that I bought last year when I was visiting the campus, before I knew whether I'd be accepted. I kept it in the back of my closet and didn't take it out until the day my acceptance letter came. The sun is still hidden behind the clouds, and the air is misty with the promise of rain. Even though I'm a little farther from the water now, the wind is still blowing hard and fast. The Coast Guard was right to shut down the beach, I decide; there's no way anyone should be out on the water on a day like today.

I press my fingers into the wood of the bench. It's riddled with carvings: initials with hearts around them, rough, messy surfboards. Someone took the time to carve an elaborate wave onto the widest plank. I close my eyes and run my fingers along the peaks and valleys of the wave, imagining that I'm on a board, flying over it, my hair streaming behind me, my stance steadier than it's ever been in real life, my heart racing as the wave begins to curl over my head.

"Ow!" I shout, bringing my finger to my mouth. I open my eyes and see that my fingertip is bleeding; I must have hit a splinter in the wood. I lean down, studying the bench, as though it will make a difference if I can figure out just which piece of wood cut me.

And that's when I see it, carved messily onto the seat beside me: *JD* and *MD*, like they were sitting right next to me.

I stand up suddenly, my pulse quickening. They sat in this very spot where I'm sitting, waiting for the same bus I'm waiting for, breathing the very air I'm breathing.

A clue. This whole summer, everything that I thought was a dead end—Kensington, the Jolly Roger, this bench—they've all been a series of *clues*. And every one has brought me one step closer.

Maybe Jas is right; we just need to keep watching the weather, following the waves, collecting these clues. Maybe, all along, my brothers have been sending me on an elaborate scavenger hunt, a game of hide-and-seek, just like we used to play when we were little. Well, then, *ready or not, here I come.*

Now my duffel bag feels light as a feather when I leave the bench behind and begin sprinting back the way I came.

Jas's truck is still in the parking lot; he hasn't left yet. I bang on the door to our motel room so hard that later my knuckles will be sore and bruised. I don't care. I'm like Jas: it would take a lot more than a few bumps and bruises to keep me out of the water now.

He opens the door and I leap into his arms like a character out of some romantic movie. I press my face into his neck and let him lift me off the ground, duffel bag and all. It feels like he's strong enough to carry me for miles.

I pull back just enough to kiss him, and when he kisses me back I think I've never tasted anything so delicious.

"Yes," I say finally, hugging him tight.

"Yes?" Jas echoes. It sounds like he can't believe that I'm really here, right now, in his arms, let alone that I'm really coming with him.

I kiss him again and then I say, "Yes." I don't think I've ever packed so much meaning into a single syllable: *Yes,* I'll come with you. *Yes,* I'll watch you ride every wave the ocean has to offer. *Yes,* you can hold my hand and open car doors and lead the way. *Yes,* together we can find my brothers.

Yes, I want to be with you, too.

32

I'M NOT SURE EXACTLY WHEN I FALL ASLEEP, BUT before I know it, Jas is shaking me awake for the second time today.

"Wake up, Darling," he says. I like the way my name sounds in his deep voice. "I'm surfing Witch Tree today."

"What?" I ask groggily. "Did the Coast Guard open the harbor?"

Jas shakes his head. "I found a captain who'll take me out."

I smile as I rub the sleep from my eyes. "I thought you were done living outside the law."

"These are once-in-a-lifetime waves, Wendy. I'm not about to miss them."

Unsurprised, I nod. "What about a tow partner?" I ask, remembering the Jet Ski waiting in the back of Jas's truck.

Jas groans. "I know," he says. "I thought for sure I'd be able to find some stragglers hanging out around the harbor, but everyone left."

I shake my head, remembering what Pete said a few hours ago.

"Not everyone," I say.

· · · · ·

It's early afternoon by the time we're on the tiny boat, heading out to sea. Jas asked if I wanted to stay on shore, but I said no way.

"I'm not going to tell you not to come," he said, "but I want to make sure that you know how dangerous it is."

"When I said yes, I meant it," I countered. "I'm coming with you. I'm through standing on the sidelines."

Jas nodded, grinning. "Yes, you are," he agreed.

Once Belle saw that I was going, she insisted on coming, too. She even brought her board along for the ride, though Pete made her promise she'd stay in the boat if conditions looked too rough once we got out there. She agreed, but I could tell by the glint in her eye—the same as the glint in Pete's eye when he accepted Jas's offer to be his tow partner for the day—there was no way she was missing this wave either.

Jas rides the Jet Ski across the boat's wake; visibility is so bad that every few minutes he disappears into the fog entirely even though he can't be more than a few yards away. The boat rushes over the chop; we bounce so hard that my teeth chatter. I'm freezing in my sweatshirt and jeans, soaked through. Belle, Pete, and Jas are all wearing wet suits and neoprene flotation vests. Back on dry land, it may be the middle of the summer, but out here, it's as cold as December.

It's like the storm that's bringing these waves is a winter storm that just lost its way.

Jas shouts at us from the Jet Ski; he nearly flipped over, and the captain has to slow the boat as Jas struggles to right himself. Our small boat is tossed from side to side as we wait. When I first saw it, bouncing in the chop by the harbor, it didn't look like much more than a rowboat with an engine attached to its hull. Once we were on board, I saw that it was, in fact, a fishing boat. It reeks of dead fish and is covered in seagull droppings. There's a small space belowdecks where the captain must live. It's no wonder that he was willing to take Jas's bribe; with the harbor closed to fishermen, Jas was his only chance at making any money today.

He gives us the thumbs-up, and the captain takes off again. I can't help wondering just what in the world is worth all this trouble. With the conditions as bad as they are, it takes us almost two hours just to get to the wave. We're already risking our lives, and no one's even tried to surf yet.

Suddenly, the captain cuts the motor—not that the boat keeps still. We're rocking back and forth, drifting out to sea. Jas pulls up alongside and offers Pete the first ride.

"We're there?" I ask. How can they even tell that we're in the right place?

Pete grins as he jumps into the water beside the boat. Jas tosses him the towrope, Pete slides his feet into his foot straps, and they take off.

"Just wait," Belle says. I'm surprised to see her standing close beside me. She's grinning so hard that her cheeks must hurt. I've never seen her look so . . . happy.

Jas pulls Pete, who stands on his board like it's a water ski. It's at least three feet shorter than the board he uses to surf back at Kensington, with rubber foot straps to hold his feet in place.

At first, I don't recognize the wave rising to the right of the boat; it looks less like the beginning of a wave and more like a monster of a whale rising to the surface.

Then it begins to grow from a lump into a hill, from a hill into a mountain, from a mountain into a wall.

Jas stops the Jet Ski and Pete sits straddling his board. Even though their backs are to me I know that they're studying the curve of the wave, deciding just where to drop in, just when Pete should let go of the towrope, just which direction Jas should turn the Jet Ski to avoid getting caught when the wave crashes down.

It seems like hours have passed by the time the wave finally begins to curl over and collapse upon itself, right back into the water. The spray reaches us even here; I'm as soaked as if I'd been the one to dive into the ocean. I lick my lips and taste salt.

As the wave begins to build again, Jas restarts the Jet Ski, expertly pulling Pete behind him. Witch Tree is not a pretty wave; the water is green and murky, not crystal clear like the water in Hawaii or luminously blue like the water down the coast. As the wave grows, its face becomes choppy, rather than smooth and glassy like the waves in Kensington.

The wave rises and I wait for it to crest, wait for Pete to let go of the towrope. But Jas keeps pulling him and the wave keeps growing, even bigger this time than the last.

The sun finally, finally breaks through the clouds, illuminating the ocean. At once, the air is crystal clear. This wave doesn't resemble any wave I've seen before. It doesn't even seem *related* to the waves that wash up on the shores of Newport Beach. I don't think I've ever seen a wave grow higher than ten feet; this wave that builds to twenty, thirty, fifty feet is a different animal entirely.

When Pete finally releases the towrope and drops into the wave, it looks like he's free-falling down the face of a cliff. It looks like madness. It looks like lunacy.

But it also looks like grace.

I don't think I could turn away if I wanted to; it's as if a magnet is pulling my gaze ever closer to the wave. Pete was made to do this; so was Jas, and maybe my brothers, too.

Pete comes flying out the side of the wave, and Jas circles back to pick him up out of the water. Even from here, even over the sound of the wave crashing and the wind howling, I can hear them shouting. They look more excited than little kids on Christmas morning.

Jas takes the wave next. He flies down the face of it, the water almost black beneath him, except for the white line of foam trailing behind his board. He holds his arms out wide, his left hand flat against the wave behind him as though it's solid as a wall. But then I guess that's exactly what it is: a wall of water. A skyscraper right here in the middle of the sea. His black hair shines in the sunlight, and his ride seems to last for hours as the wave continues to lengthen out in front of us. Pete whoops from his place on the Jet Ski; he keeps a close watch so that he can pull Jas out of the soup once his ride is over.

"Maybe they *are* superheroes," I say out loud.

"What?" Belle asks.

I shake my head. "Just something I was thinking earlier. Like they are two superheroes fighting for world domination."

Belle laughs, surprising me. "Yeah, and look what they can do when they join forces," she says as the wave curls over Jas's head, crashing into the ocean with a deafening roar. Pete grabs Jas from the water before the foam gets too thick.

The wave begins to build again, and I wonder who will take the next ride. The boat rocks jerkily from side to side.

My parents spent their honeymoon on a yacht in the South Pacific; my father once told me that sleeping out on the open water, the waves lapping the side of the boat, was like being rocked to sleep in an enormous cradle. The memory makes me want to laugh out loud. Being on this boat is like being held in the jaws of some wild animal, the kind that whips its prey back and forth, stunning it before it kills it. I watch the wave rise and fall as though I'm possessed by it, until it feels like it's coming from someplace deep inside of me, until I can't remember, no matter how hard I try, what it feels like to stand on solid ground.

Beside me, Belle is picking up her own board. "My turn now," she says, waving at the boys to come back to the boat for her.

"Good luck," I shout as she jumps overboard.

33

JAS PUTS HIS ARMS AROUND ME AS WE WATCH PETE tow Belle away from the boat.

"You must be freezing," he says, rubbing my arms up and down with his enormous hands.

I shake my head. Much to my surprise, I feel warm; I'm sweating. Adrenaline is pumping through my body. I wonder how many waves there will be like this one, how many times I'll get to watch Jas surf the latest behemoth the ocean offers up.

"I can't wait," I say out loud, and Jas kisses the top of my head, understanding exactly what I mean.

As Pete pulls Belle into the wave, the sun slips behind the clouds and it begins to rain. But even from here I can see that Belle isn't about to stop. Not when she's so close.

"That girl has guts," Jas says, a hint of pride in his voice. "I can count on one hand the number of girls in the world who are strong enough to take that wave."

"Hey!" I say, elbowing him in the ribs. "Don't knock girl surfers."

Jas shakes his head solemnly. "I'm not," he says as he pulls the hood of my sweatshirt over my head. "Just the opposite."

The second that Belle lets go of the towrope, the skies open; what was a drizzle is now a downpour. I suppose the rain really doesn't matter; we're all so soaked already. But without the sun, visibility is all but nonexistent.

I have to concentrate to see Belle's blond hair streaking across the face of the wave. If the tip of the wave weren't white with foam, I wouldn't be able to see the moment when the water shifts, crashing down on top of her with a speed and a force that shock me, as though the wave is a living thing with a mind set on shoving Belle from its surface.

Belle flips off of her board, head over heels. Pete tries to turn the Jet Ski, but somehow the wave is still pounding down. Pete can't drive directly into its center, where Belle is currently getting worked. Jas and I watch in silence, keeping our eyes trained on the spot where Belle's blond head keeps disappearing and reappearing.

The surface of the water is completely white with foam, and Pete drives the Jet Ski dangerously close. Jas explains that a Jet Ski simply can't drive over soup; in foamy conditions the engine isn't able to get enough water to propel itself forward.

"He's going to stall if he's not careful," Jas says stonily. But he and I both know: nothing is going to keep Pete from getting to Belle. Jas leans over the bow of the boat, his feet poised to spring.

"Wait!" I say desperately, but it's too late, he's already gone, swimming toward the wave. The ocean is so loud that I don't think he could have heard me anyway.

Jas makes his way out to where Pete is waiting on the Jet Ski, just outside the impact zone of the wave. He climbs on just as Pete dives off and begins swimming toward Belle. Slowly, carefully, Jas directs the Jet Ski to follow.

It seems like hours have passed before Pete gets to Belle and is able to pull her out of the soup and onto the Jet Ski. Jas takes off in the direction of the boat, leaving Pete behind to try to swim his way out of there.

"Here," Jas shouts; he barely stops the Jet Ski as he heaves Belle in my direction. I fit my hands underneath her armpits and pull her up onto the deck. She moans softly. Jas circles back for Pete, and together they scramble onto the boat, leaving the Jet Ski behind.

"Go!" Pete shouts at the captain.

"What about the Jet Ski?" I ask dumbly, looking out at the sea. Belle's board is left out there somewhere, too.

"Forget it," Jas says, kneeling down beside Belle. It's then that I see that the deck is covered in blood. The right leg of Belle's wet suit is slashed open and blood is pouring from the opening.

"Oh my god," I say softly.

"The fin of her board must have sliced her," Jas says.

He and Pete are working together, tying towels around her leg to stanch the bleeding. Now I'm freezing; I can't stop shaking. The motor roars and spits as the boat takes off, the captain navigating his way through the chop, desperately trying to lead us back to shore. But ten, twenty, even thirty minutes have passed, and we've barely moved. I can still hear the roar of Witch Tree behind us. Smaller but still massive waves rise in front of us. It feels like we're trapped between mountains.

Jas pulls me down onto the deck beside him and puts his arm around me. Pete shifts Belle's leg in his lap, pressing his hands tightly over her wound. I think if he could wrap his whole body around her to apply more pressure, he would.

"What do we do?" I whisper to Jas. Belle looks small and pale, and the pool of blood beneath her leg continues to grow; Pete's grip and the soaked towels we tied around her haven't made a bit of difference. Jas shakes his head.

Belle moans; softly at first, and then louder. "Just the same," she says. "Just the same."

"Shhh, Belle," Pete murmurs. "Just hang on a little bit longer."

But Belle shakes her head and struggles to sit up. Her eyes flutter open and she looks right at me.

"Just the same," she says, and it seems that it takes every ounce of her strength to speak. There is something she's determined to say, and I know enough about Belle to know that once she makes up her mind to do something, she will do it, even when each breath she takes is an effort. I'm surprised to realize that it's something we have in common, that look that we get on our faces when we're absolutely determined to do something, the look that Jas recognized when he watched me surf on my own.

So I ask, "What's just the same, Belle?"

"The ocean," she says. "Same today as it was *that* day."

"What day?" I ask.

Belle's gray eyes haven't lost any of their steel; they lock with mine as she says, "The day that your brothers went missing."

I feel like a balloon someone has just sliced open; all the air goes out of me and I'm not sure I'll ever be able to take a breath again.

"I was there," she says, struggling on every word. "Six months ago. I was there. *Here*. They were on dust," she says, her eyes flickering from my face to Jas's.

"They surfed Witch Tree on dust?" Pete says, incredulous. "You can't even surf Kensie on dust."

Belle nods weakly. "I tried to stop them," she whispers; I can barely hear her above the wind and the rain. "I swear I tried. But they wouldn't listen."

She's crying; or maybe that's the rain on her face. I can't tell whether the water on my face is coming from inside of me anymore either.

"I almost told you," she adds. "Before you left our house, I almost told you, but I just couldn't." She shakes her head. "Just couldn't," she repeats, her unspoken apology floating in the mist between us.

I almost laugh at the idea of this girl, this powerhouse who didn't hesitate before she splashed into the ocean today, unable to tell me anything.

"I watched them," she says, desperately. "I kept my eyes on them every second, until . . ."

The words she doesn't say hang in the air; she watched them every second until she couldn't watch them anymore. Until they disappeared. I shake my head, thinking about the figures I saw on the beach last night, the voices I heard. They must have been ghosts.

Carefully, pressing against the soaked deck and then grabbing at the side of the boat, I stand up. The boat is heaving and pitching; the captain shouts at me from his place behind the controls.

"Sit down, Wendy," Jas says, reaching for me. "It's not safe."

I shake my head, carefully backing away from him. I have to keep my hands gripping the edge of the boat to keep from falling as the ocean tosses us around like it's a wild mustang and we're fools to ride it. The captain keeps shouting, pointing at something behind me. I begin to turn; a wave twice the size of any I've ever seen is building in front of me. It must be one hundred feet tall and climbing.

My brothers are dead. Jas and I can search every wave around the world, we can follow every swell: we will never find them. They vanished six months ago, just like everyone said. I was wrong to believe I could find them and bring them home, more wrong than anyone has ever been about anything. More wrong than Jas was to sell them the drugs, more wrong than Pete was to lie to me, more wrong than Belle was to hide the truth.

I let go.

· · · · ·

The first thing I feel is the cold. I thought I was cold on the boat, but this is something else entirely. It's a cold that shocks me to my very bones, blinding me so that I can't even see the boat anymore. I wonder just how far the wave flung me. For a second, before I hit the water, it felt like I was flying.

Water is not soft on impact. It's as hard as stone against my skin. Instinct has me struggling to stay on the surface of the water, wrestling with the waves that plunge me down deep, over and over.

I flail my arms desperately; soon I can't tell which way is up. Maybe I'm swimming deeper when I think I'm swimming for the surface. I open my mouth to gasp for oxygen, genuinely surprised to find that I'm underwater, and instead of air, my mouth is filling with liquid.

I wonder how long I can hold my breath. I've always heard that in situations like this, you discover that you can survive without oxygen for longer than you ever imagined.

Belle and Pete and Jas all swam in this water before me and survived; but then they had their flotation vests on and all I have is this sweatshirt that feels like it weighs a thousand pounds.

How long did my brothers fight in this water? How long were they able to hold their breath? Did they stay together or did the waves drive them apart? Did one of them drown first? Did the other have to watch, helpless, as the person he was closest to on the planet disappeared under the water for the last time? Are they here now, floating somewhere beneath me, waiting for me to join them?

Suddenly, I want to swim down, down, down, into the depths of the icy water below me. There is still one way I can find my brothers, even if I can't bring them home the way I planned. But I can join them. I throw my hands above my head, trying to propel myself deeper.

Then someone is grabbing me, pulling me higher.

"Hang on to me," Jas says, his voice thick. He must have jumped in after me. Of course he jumped in after me.

He's holding me tighter than I've ever been held before.

"Hang on to me," he says again, but I can't seem to make my arms wind around him, can't make my fingers hold on. Maybe they're frozen from the cold or maybe they just don't want to. Maybe my body has already made up its mind; it's ready to let go.

My head slips beneath the surface again, and Jas struggles to pull me up.

I picture my lungs filling with water every time I go under, just a little more each time. Who knew it was possible to drown so gradually?

I hear Jas each time I resurface.

"I'm sorry," he says.

"I love you," he says.

"I'll spend the rest—"

Then I don't hear anything anymore.

34

I'VE BEEN AWAKE FOR A WHILE NOW, BUT I HAVEN'T opened my eyes yet. I'm not sure I want to open my eyes ever again. I try to force myself back to sleep, but it's so noisy that I wonder how I ever slept here at all. There is the beep of some machine near my head that seems to be registering my pulse, the sound of footsteps, an echo of laughter, and, from somewhere nearby, an urgent call for a nurse.

I'm in a hospital. That much is obvious. I can feel an IV stuck into my left arm. My entire body aches, and my neck feels so stiff that I don't think I can turn my head; I'll learn later that my collarbone is broken, along with several ribs.

It's my lungs that give me away; I try to take a deep breath and instead begin coughing violently. My lungs still feel like they're full of water.

I wonder just how close I came to drowning. I hear footsteps rushing in, a nurse coming to check on me.

I open my eyes.

"Well hello there, sleepyhead," the nurse says in an overly cheerful voice. Her scrubs are pink with little teddy bears running down the middle. Maybe I'm in the pediatric unit.

I open my mouth to speak, but I can't stop coughing. The nurse hands me a plastic cup of water, and I shake my head. Water is the last thing I need. I need someone to stick their hands down my throat and wring out my water-soaked lungs. But that's not, obviously, an option, so I reach for the cup. That's when I discover that my arms are in restraints. Loosely, but still. I look accusingly at the nurse, sweat beading up at the back of my neck despite the fact that the room is cool.

"I'll untie that for you," the nurse says obligingly, undoing the restraint around my right arm. She watches as I drink. I empty the cup slowly, scared that the minute I finish she's going to tie me back up.

But instead she says she's going to get my parents. Her tone seems to imply that she'll be back in just a minute, so it's not worth my trying anything. I get the feeling this is some kind of test to see what I'll do with my new freedom. So I don't untie my other wrist.

My parents come in, walking in step like soldiers marching into battle. They don't rush to hug me; instead they stand at the foot of my bed, like they're scared that if they touch me I'll break.

"Where am I exactly?" I ask. I don't bother saying hello.

The water is the last thing I remember. Jas's arms around me. He must have gotten me back to the boat somehow; they must have made it back to the harbor and rushed us to the hospital. I must have swallowed too much water, lost consciousness.

"You're in the hospital," my mother says.

I glance at my left arm, still tightly bound by restraints. I don't think I'm in the pediatric wing after all.

"Where exactly in the hospital am I?" I ask.

My mother glances at the nurse and bites her lip.

"Mom?" I prompt.

It's the nurse who speaks, but by the time she does, the answer has already become clear: I'm in the psych ward. She calls it "the psychiatric unit," but we both know that's just a euphemism.

I try to sit up, the loose hospital pajamas I'm wearing rustling like they're made of paper. "Why am I tied up?"

"You kept trying to run away," my mother blurts out, then looks apologetically at the nurse. The nurse comes and sits on the edge of my bed and takes my hand in hers. I have to resist the urge to glance accusingly at my parents; this is their job, not some stranger's, to sit beside me and comfort me.

"You've been unconscious for days. We think you were having something like nightmares. Do you remember what you saw?"

I shake my head.

"You called out names, insisted that you had to go back and make sure they were okay. You kept trying to get up. We finally had to restrain you, just to help you stay put."

She laughs as she says the last words, like she's trying to make the restraints seem cute. Like I was a kid falling out of bed and they didn't want me to hurt myself.

"Do you remember what names you called?"

I shake my head, though I can guess. Belle is probably somewhere in this hospital, too, her leg wrapped in bandages, crisscrossed with stitches. Maybe Jas is waiting outside; maybe they wouldn't let him in because he's not family.

"Can I see them?" I ask finally.

"See who?"

"Belle," I say, wincing at the memory of the bloody gash in her leg. "I'll go to her room if she can't be moved. And Pete and Jas."

The nurse cocks her head to the side, the same way Nana does when she doesn't know what I'm talking about. Evidently, the names have no meaning to her, beyond being the names I cried out in the night.

"Come on," I say, begging. "The people who brought me here. The people who were on the boat with me."

"What boat, Wendy?"

"*The* boat. The only boat that was stupid enough to go out on the water."

My parents look desperately at the nurse, as though they believe she has all the answers. I narrow my eyes, staring at her. Nurses wear name tags, and this woman doesn't. And I don't think she's the type to have forgotten it at home.

I sit up, the remaining restraint tightening around my left wrist, the muscles in my back aching in protest. "What's your name?" I ask.

"Mary," she answers.

"Are you a nurse?"

She shakes her head. "No," she says. "I'm your doctor, Wendy. Your therapist."

I nod; I think I knew that.

"Wendy," Mary continues, her voice frustratingly calm, a

perfectly rehearsed monotone. "You were found on the sand near Pebble Beach; you'd tried to swim out into the storm, but the water was just too rough."

I shake my head. "That's not what happened," I begin to say.

But Mary continues. "You were found just down the beach from where the police found your brothers' surfboards. Were you looking for John and Michael?"

"Yes," I say too quickly. "I mean, no. I mean, when I went there, I thought that maybe I could find them."

My parents exchange a look. Each time I glance their way they seem more stricken than the last.

I shake my head. "But I know that they drowned out there. I understand that now."

Mary lowers her achingly calm voice like we're about to share a secret. "Did you think you could join them?"

I open my mouth to say no, but I close it before any words can come out. Because I remember being in the water, shivering in the cold, believing that I might be able to find them still, if I just let myself sink.

"Wendy," Mary says, "we don't have to cover everything today. You're awake, you're coherent, you're not trying to run." She leans over and unties the restraint, but my left arm stays resting on the bed. "That's better isn't it?" she says, like she's done me some huge favor.

"Wait," I say, desperate. Somehow Mary took control of this conversation, changed the subject on me. I try to get it back on track. "Belle, Pete, Jas, the captain—where are they? The boat made it back to the harbor, didn't it?"

Mary looks at me blankly, barely even blinking as the words

tumble out of my mouth. I try to explain: I went out with my friends that day, to watch them surf. Conditions were rough. Belle got hurt. I got thrown overboard.

My heart is pounding in my chest.

Mary just shakes her head firmly. "No boats were allowed out on the water that day," she says. "The Coast Guard shut the harbor down."

"I know," I answer. "We shouldn't have gone out there." Maybe I just need to sound contrite. Maybe they're just mad at me for taking the risks I took.

But then a realization washes over me, just another wave crashing over my head.

"You said I was found on the beach? No one brought me here?" Mary nods, smiling, pleased that I've begun to understand. But I know that *she's* the one who doesn't understand.

I must have drifted away somehow, far from the boat and Jas and Pete and Belle. The current carried me back to shore. That's why I was shouting for them in my sleep, begging to go back and find them.

I sit up quickly, so fast that it startles Mary, who backs away from me, her hands out in front of her as though she thinks I might hurt her. But instead I stand. My broken bones shoot pain through my body defiantly and my legs wobble underneath me, as though the muscles have forgotten how to hold me up. I wonder just how long I was lying in that bed.

"Where are my clothes?" I ask, looking not at Mary but at my parents. "Come on," I plead. "We have to go. They haven't even looked for them. They might be alive." Surely my parents at least will spring into action once they understand: a boat is missing with four people on it. Send out the Coast Guard, search and rescue, the National Guard, whoever takes over at times like this.

But my parents avoid my gaze, and I don't see Mary press the little yellow button she wears tucked into the waistband of her pants. Later, I'll learn that it's called a panic button. Today, I just learn that when she presses it, people much stronger than I am enter the room and force me back into the bed.

I struggle at first. I call for Belle; she'd be strong enough to escape these guys, even with the gash in her leg. I shout the word *Kensington*, the word *Pete*, the words *Witch Tree*. I try to shout Jas's name, but the word gets caught behind the lump in my throat, choking me. By the time they're tying the restraints around my wrists again, I've lost the strength to fight anymore.

Finally, I ask, "What do you mean, something *like* nightmares?"

Mary doesn't blink, doesn't break eye contact for a second, before she says the word *hallucinations*.

Where the restraints touch my wrists, my skin burns like it's on fire.

35

IT TAKES A FEW DAYS FOR THE DETAILS TO BECOME clear. I was found on the beach near where my brothers' boards were discovered months ago; the doctors think I made some kind of deluded attempt to find my brothers by joining them at the bottom of the sea.

I was unconscious when they found me, and drifted in and out of consciousness for days, calling for Pete, for Belle, for Jas. Mary and the other doctors think those names are attached to people who don't exist outside of my imagination.

We've been through this before, I want to shout. But instead, I keep calm each time I explain, telling my story over and over again, begging them to call the Coast Guard. I feel like a murder suspect being grilled under bright, hot lights, like they're trying to catch me in a lie, to poke holes in my story. Which, of course, they are. They think that once they break my story apart, I'll see that it simply can't have been possible.

They also can't agree on whether it was drug-induced

psychosis or grief-induced psychosis. It's a little *which came first, the chicken or the egg.* Did I take the drugs because I was so grief-stricken and then manufacture this world, or did I manufacture this world because I was so grief-stricken and take drugs to keep the illusion alive?

They say it's unlikely that I took the drugs only once, like I think that I did. They insist that it's unlikely it was a single drug; there are still traces of different hallucinogens in my system now—a cocktail of rare chemicals so obscure that they don't even have street names. They don't seem to care about where I got the drugs or how they came to be combined the way they did. They don't believe me that it was only one drug that was made up of all those different ones. They think I took them each separately, over a period of weeks and months, stretching all the way back to my high school graduation, until the drugs all mingled in my system and wreaked havoc on my psyche.

No one believes me about the boat, about the way Pete and Belle and Jas rode the wave, even as the storm threatened to sink us all. They tell me it wouldn't have been possible for anyone to surf that wave.

I'm embarrassed, at first, to tell them that I was in love with at least one—if not two—of my illusions, but they figure it out. It is their job to be insightful, after all. Something about the way I look when I talk about Pete, about the way my voice catches in my throat every single time I try to say Jas's name, gives me away. They tell me that these relationships were the biggest illusion of all, because they were the part to which I was most attached. Emotionally.

On that point, at least, I don't argue.

. . . . .

Because of all my injuries, I go to physical therapy in another wing of the hospital every day, but no one tries to deny that the real reason I'm here is for psychotherapy. After all, I could do the physical therapy as an outpatient. In their soothing voices—I soon discover that Mary isn't the only one here who's mastered that aggravatingly calm monotone—they tell me that my delusion was my way of confronting my brothers' deaths: I was in such deep denial that my subconscious had to create a reality in which I saw, plain as day, the reality of their deaths, a reality in which I not only saw but felt exactly how they died.

In our family sessions, my mother cries that it's all her fault. She let her one remaining child slip away. Eventually my father, Mary the therapist, and I find ourselves comforting her, reassuring her. I can't blame my mother for being so shocked; who would have thought that Wendy, her Goody Two-shoes, would have turned out to be a crazy, drug-addled runaway?

The day I refer to my time in Kensington as an illusion is the first time in a long time that I see my mother smile. When I said it, I didn't actually mean anything by it, didn't mean to imply that I accepted their theories about my madness. I only said *illusion* because it's easier to use the same language they use.

But the word makes my mother so happy that I say it again the next time I see her, and again the next. At first, the word tastes sour in my mouth, but slowly the bitterness fades, until the word doesn't taste like anything at all. I say it so many times that I get used to it, never entirely sure whether I believe it or not, never quite sure that what I believe matters.

Once I say it enough times, they let me go home.

The first morning I wake up in my room at home, I don't recognize it. I open my eyes expecting to be on a mattress on the floor in Pete's house. Then, I swear I can feel Jas's arms around me, smell the sea, feel the salt air on my skin. But instead of a run-down motel on the beach, I'm in the glass house on the hill. Instead of the ocean, the view from my window is the city lights, fading beneath the sunrise.

I have to beg, but one day my parents finally take me to the beach. Mary said it would be okay; she said it might be good for me. Not anywhere near Kensington, of course. No, the beach nearest our house, the one where we had the bonfire the night I graduated. A night that seems a million years ago.

"Why did you want to come here so much?" my mother asks, but I don't answer her because I'm too busy watching the surfers take to the water. There are at least a dozen here that I can see, scattered beyond the break of the waves, taking turns paddling into surf that doesn't rise higher than six feet. There was a time when waves like this would have seemed enormous to me, but now they seem small.

At home, I've been Googling big-wave surfing and watching video after video of surfers dropping into mammoth waves. One afternoon, my father found me hypnotized by videos of surfers at Teahupoo. At first, he seemed all set to call Mary, report a relapse, readmit me to the hospital. But after a few seconds, he was sitting beside me, just as riveted as I was by the images of someone flying inside the tunnel of the powerful wave.

"Its name means 'broken skulls,'" I said without thinking.

My father didn't ask me how I knew that, and I'm not sure I

could have told him if he had. Instead, he studied the way the wave crashed into the ocean, the way the barrel narrowed at its edges, so that even the most skilled surfer had trouble making it out of the tunnel without being pummeled by the water crashing down around him.

After a few minutes, my father said, "I can see how it got that name."

Now he puts his arm around me gently. He seems almost as fascinated by the surfers here as I am. I wonder if he's thinking of John and Michael, of the years they spent surfing this beach before they ran off in search of bigger and better waves.

If my parents were to forbid me from ever picking up a surfboard, I would understand why. How could they be sure that I wouldn't disappear just like John and Michael, drawn in by the waves' siren song?

But much to my surprise, my father says, "Feels good to be back on the beach, doesn't it?"

I nod. "It does."

"We'll have to start coming here more often," he says carefully. For a second, my mother looks stricken, but slowly, unexpectedly, a smile spreads across her face.

I think she must feel the same way I do. Like me, she feels closest to John and Michael when she's near the water.

36

I GET VERY GOOD AT WAITING. I WAIT AS I DUTIFULLY go to my outpatient therapy with Mary each week, talk about my feelings and answer questions and go through the five stages of grief for my brothers like I'm checking them off a to-do list. I wait until Fiona can laugh when I joke that I'm finally seeing a grief counselor, just like she wanted me to months ago. I wait until I can honestly say that the counseling helps; she was right after all. I wait until my parents have agreed that I can start college in January; they've ironed everything out with Stanford, I'll just matriculate one semester late. I wait until my mother lets me take the car and drive myself to therapy, alone. I wait until she's actually sent me out on errands by myself: pick up a dozen eggs, the dry cleaning, a tube of toothpaste. I wait until the weather turns cooler and the days are shorter, until I can speak about my brothers in the past tense without tripping over the words. I wait until my parents trust me. Only then do I take the car—a fresh, new, shiny SUV my parents bought for me to take to college, a belated graduation gift, so normal and unsurprising—and drive to Kensington Beach.

I drive there because I have to see it for myself. I drive there because even now, all this time later, I wake up every morning and think I'm somewhere else. Every morning, I think I'm in Kensington.

· · · · ·

The roads are familiar, but that doesn't necessarily mean anything. Mary and her colleagues all conceded that I probably did make my way to the gated community that was once called Kensington Beach at some point during my psychosis. Fiona Googled the place and told me what I already knew: that it was a popular beachside housing development in the 1980s but had long since been abandoned. No one lives there now. It's not safe. The only reason they haven't torn the houses down is the cliffs aren't stable enough for tractors and trailers to park there, let alone lug away debris. The place itself is unstable. Just like me.

Now I wonder how I found it; my GPS stops working short of the turn that leads me up the cliffs. In fact, according to my GPS, I'm driving straight into the ocean.

I pull into the driveway of what would have been Jas's house. It's there, just like I remember it, but instead of looking like it received a fresh coat of paint a few months ago, the exterior of the house is beat-up, the paint peeling and chipped. There's graffiti all over the garage door, and when I try the front door, prepared to break a window to get inside if I have to, it's unlocked.

The house is empty. There isn't a single piece of furniture

inside. There's more graffiti on the interior walls, but it's completely illegible. On one wall, someone has drawn a surfer taking a massive wave. It looks exactly like the picture I saw on the bench when I waited for the bus. There's some trash on the floor. I take a deep breath, as though maybe there will be some trace of the scents I associate with Jas, but the place smells vaguely of stale beer and pot, like maybe some kids crashed here while they surfed the waves on the beach below. Or maybe they were just looking for a place to party, completely unaware of the waves at all.

At least the house is shaped like I remember it, a mirror image of Pete's, perched on the cliffs on the other side of Kensington. I head for the garage, remembering the collection of surfboards I saw there the first time I saw Jas. Maybe there will be some trace of him there at least.

But there is nothing; just another empty room.

I walk out through the front door and head down the overgrown road that will lead to Pete's house. When I see it, I break into a run. Maybe some of Pete's crew still lives here; maybe Hughie or Matt is waiting just on the other side of the door.

But the house is a mess; it reeks of mildew, as if a wave rose up from the ocean below and drenched the place. The sliding glass doors that lead to the backyard are wide open; a few seagulls are hopping around the living room. They've made this house their home. The tile floors that were always gleamingly white, where Pete laid out a blanket and we all ate the dinner I cooked, are covered with feathers and droppings. The birds caw at me in protest as I make my way to the backyard, toward the one thing here that's familiar: the sound of the waves.

The cliffs fall so straight and so sharp that I take a step back, afraid I might fall. The rocks are jagged and toothlike. It'd be impossible to build stairs into these cliffs. And I can't imagine why anyone would want to.

Because below me, there is no beach. The water comes right up to the cliffs. There is no perfect triangle of white sand. The waves are rough and choppy, driving themselves directly into the wall of rocks, spray colliding with stone. To surf them would be certain death.

It's as if the ocean has swallowed my memories whole.

• • • • •

I stop at Fiona's on the drive home. I'd told my parents that I was going there when I left the house this morning, and of course they believed me, now that I'm back to normal.

Fiona's home from school for the weekend—she left for college at the usual time in September, like everyone else—and after months away, she's thrilled to see me out on my own.

"You look so good, Wen," she squeals as we hug hello.

I laugh, but Fiona shakes her head.

"No, I mean seriously. I don't know, ever since this summer . . . I mean, you even looked pretty that morning you showed up here, stoned out of your mind."

"Now I know you're just being nice."

"I'm not," Fiona insists. "Really."

I put my arms around my best friend and hug her again as she oohs and aahs over my new car. I let her drive it down from her house in the hills when we go out to dinner. I roll the windows down and breathe in the scent of the eucalyptus trees that line her neighborhood, erasing any trace of the ocean.

I'm tempted to apologize to her, to tell her she was right all along. But instead I listen as she tells me about her breakup with Dax, about the cute guy who lives on her floor in the dorm, about the professor she has a crush on, about the sorority she's decided to pledge.

"Not," she adds quickly, like she's worried it might upset me, "that I'll ever know any of those girls the way I know you."

I'm not sure *I* know me anymore. I'd been so certain that my summer in the sun was real, so certain that Fiona and Mary and my parents were wrong.

I was supposed to be a detective hunting for clues, but it turns out that my brain just constructed some kind of elaborate scavenger hunt for me, the same way I used to do for my brothers.

I close my eyes and remember the day that Fiona and I met in kindergarten; we were instant friends because we were both wearing the same purple striped shirt. We held hands on our first day of high school, terrified of the seniors, all of whom seemed a foot taller than we were. I remember the day Fiona passed her driver's test and the first day of our senior year, the way we walked side by side, giggling because now the freshmen seemed so small. I can still hear the catch of pride in her voice the first time she called Dax her boyfriend, and I can still feel the way she hugged me tight even when she thought I was losing my mind. Which it turns out, I kind of was. I smile. I have plenty of memories that *are* real.

Poor Fee was right all along. I guess she really does know me best. She saw right away that I'd made up Kensington, Pete,

Belle, Jas. All the money my parents spent on therapy and doctors, all that analysis to discover that I'd created a world where I could put off mourning my brothers because I was too busy falling in love and being loved, until my fantasy brought me to Witch Tree and finally began coming apart at the seams. I needed to see what my brothers saw; I even invented someone revealing their death to me. Fiona could have explained it all for free.

I reach across the front seat to squeeze Fiona's hand on my fresh new steering wheel. I have a best friend who is real, who loves me, who tried to save me when I was going mad. I don't need Pete and Belle; I don't need Jas. I have something real right here.

"Of course not," I answer finally. I pause, the beginning of a smile tugging at the corners of my mouth. "I think you might actually know me better than I know myself."

37

DRIVING HOME LATER, I WONDER WHAT MARY would say if she knew I went to Kensington today, if she knew that now I've seen what's really there. Mary would argue—she *has* argued—that I have every right to mourn the loss of Jas and Pete and Belle and Kensington and the life I thought I knew there. She'd say since they had all been real to me, I ought to grieve for them now that they're gone. It's the kind of logic I've always hated. You shouldn't be able to have feelings for things that aren't real. Or for people who aren't real.

So I'm not crying over my loss as I drive down the PCH, putting miles between Kensington and me. Instead, I'm laughing. I'm laughing because I should have known all along that it wasn't real; it was so obvious, now that I think about it. I left myself such an enormous clue, right in the center of my delusion:

There's no way I ever would have really taken a wave.

By the time I get home, I've decided that I'm going to major in math when I get to Stanford. There's no such thing as imaginary numbers.

Except, of course, there are.

I go to my room and close the door. The other day my mother gave me back the notebook she'd confiscated months ago, the one in which I'd kept all my notes when I thought I was living in Pete's house. It's lying forgotten on my desk, but now I open it, run my hands over my scribbles. Even my handwriting doesn't look like my own; it's messier, somehow desperate-looking. The handwriting of a person having a mental breakdown. I slam the book shut and drop it into the trash can beneath my desk.

In therapy yesterday, Mary asked me whether I ever said *I love you* to Jas. I didn't answer her. Already my memories—or whatever I'm supposed to call what I remember of my hallucinations—are beginning to fade. They're fuzzy, like a painting onto which someone has thrown a bucket of water, the borders between each image bleeding together until they're indistinct.

She pushed me; I must have loved him, she said, if I was planning on running away with him, traveling the world with him, giving up my whole life—school, family, friends—just to be with him. I must have loved him, she said again. Didn't I?

I never actually told her that I was planning on running away with Jas. I must have said something about it when I was half-conscious, babbling endlessly, calling out in my sleep. She must have sat by my bed taking notes.

I refused to answer her. And I certainly didn't tell her that when I woke up in the psych ward months ago, my first thought was the words *I love you, too*. In the water, when he was trying to save me—when he told me he loved me—I never had a chance to say it back; the water was crashing over me so rapidly, I hardly had time to open my mouth to take a breath, let alone utter four syllables.

I decide that next week, I'll answer Mary's latest question. I'll tell her that I didn't say *I love you* to Jas because you can't love someone who doesn't exist. Whatever this ache in my chest is, it can't be the pain of missing him, because he was never here to begin with. This ache is just wasted space.

• • • • •

The next morning, as I make myself a bowl of cereal, I discover that we're out of milk. My mother will send me out to the grocery store for more later. She doesn't even think twice about sending me out on errands anymore. It's even a little annoying how quick she is to say, "Wendy, dear, can you go pick that up?"

Just a few weeks ago, that would have been such a big deal. A few weeks ago, I was excited to be sent out for milk. I smile as I eat my dry cereal, Nana's enormous head resting in my lap; that's progress, I guess.

I haven't bothered getting dressed yet today; I'm still wearing pajama pants and a shirt I stole from Michael a couple years ago, long before he and John disappeared. He used to wear it to the beach, and it got so soft and faded in the sunshine that when it was accidentally folded in with my laundry, I never gave it back. He huffed and puffed looking for this shirt, and I never confessed to him that I had it all along, tucked away at the bottom of my drawer, waiting to take it with me when I left for college, a little piece of home.

Now, at least, I don't have to hide it anymore.

I'm tossing the last of my dry cereal when my father comes bounding through the front door.

"What are you doing home?" I ask. Since I got back from the hospital, he's actually been going to work on time every day. My parents' daily routine is beginning to look more and more like it did not just before I washed up on the beach but before my brothers ran away. My mother gets up and dressed every morning, goes for a long walk with Nana around the neighborhood. My father goes to work five days a week, and even works late once in a while, just like he used to.

He doesn't answer me, just calls my mother's name. She practically skips from her bedroom to meet him, her hair still wet from her morning shower. Nana dances at her feet, giddy because my parents are giddy.

"Wendy," my dad says, barely keeping a straight face. "There's a delivery for you in the driveway."

I raise my eyebrows. They already got me a car, and that gift didn't come with nearly so much fanfare. My father and I went to the dealership together; I test drove a few models and crunched the numbers alongside my dad before we decided which was the right one for me. I drove it home myself; there wasn't any big reveal, no car waiting in the driveway with a big red bow tied around it.

What could possibly be in the driveway?

My bare feet squeak against the tile floor as I walk to the front door. A few months ago—a million years ago—I would have thought that it was my brothers, waiting there for me. I would have believed that somehow, some magic had led them back to the glass house, where they were waiting patiently in the driveway to surprise me with their presence. But today, the idea doesn't even cross my mind. My brothers are dead, and I've finally begun the long process of learning how to live without them.

The sun is bright in my eyes when I open the front door. I squint, holding one hand like a visor against my forehead. There, leaning against the side of my car, all wrapped in a big red bow, is a surfboard. I take a few tentative steps toward it, as though I think it might sprout legs and run away if I get too close too fast. I glance back at my parents, who are grinning from the doorway.

The board is beautiful. Creamy white on the sides, with fading blocks of pale green, yellow, and pink floating across its center. It's actually the perfect length for someone my height; even in my fantasies, I never actually surfed on a board that was the right size for me. Still, the new board towers over me. My father has even tied a block of wax to the board, and it dangles from a string beneath the red ribbon.

I reach out and touch it, feel the familiar texture of fiberglass, eye the sharp fins at its bottom. I turn back to my parents.

"This is for me?"

They nod, coming through the door arm in arm.

"It's for you," my father answers.

"We know how badly you want to learn to surf," my mom says. "You talked about it in family sessions all the time. And then, the other day at the beach, we just thought . . ." She pauses, chewing her lip. "We thought maybe this was something you wanted."

I nod. I think maybe I've never wanted anything as much as I want to grab this board and run with it into the waves.

"We can go to the shop later and get a rack installed for you on the roof," my father adds, gesturing to my car. "You'll need it to drive the board up to school with you."

"To school?" I echo.

He nods. "I know Stanford's not exactly on the coast, but there are plenty of beaches in driving distance."

I nod; the words he doesn't say float between us. The beach where I was found is only a couple hours' drive from Stanford.

"Just be careful," my mother begins, but my father shakes his head, silencing her.

I study my parents' faces; they're smiling, but there is such fear behind their eyes. My mother has her fingers wrapped around Nana's collar to keep her from running into the street, but she's holding on more tightly than is really necessary, like she just needs something to hang on to. I realize just how much this gesture means, what a sign it is of their trust in me, of their bravery, to push me out onto the water, where I most want to be, despite everything that happened to me and everything that happened to my brothers.

"If it's not the right height," my mother adds, "or if you don't like the color—"

I shake my head. "No," I say, a smile creeping across my lips.

I can already imagine the water beneath my beautiful board, the sensation of falling as I drop into a wave.

"It's perfect," I add, pulling my mother into a hug. "I love it."

38

JANUARY IS UNSEASONABLY WARM, EVEN FOR southern California. The forecasters on the evening news don't bother masking their surprise each time the temperature rises: seventy-three; seventy-eight; eighty-one; and, on the day I leave for college, eighty-four.

"Beach weather," my dad says carelessly as he loads my bedding into the backseat for me. I nod, glancing at my surfboard, secured tightly to the rack on the roof of my car.

I spent last night—when I should have been packing, or at least looking at my course catalog on the computer—waxing my board. I couldn't help myself. I want the board to be prepared, perfect for when the time comes. My mother has already told me that when I'm ready, they're going to treat me to surf lessons at the beach of my choice. They'll hire me a private instructor. I almost groaned when she mentioned it—what could be lamer than an expensive private teacher on the beach?—but I could see that it was important to her. She's willing to let me go out on the water, her face said, but please, please, let her have this one thing, this assurance that I'll be out there as safely as possible.

So I stifled my groan and thanked her instead.

I don't really plan to head to the water anytime soon, despite the unseasonable warmth. I'm honestly excited to start classes, to have a schedule, to study and write papers. It's been so long that I'm worried I may have forgotten how.

My dad startles me by taking a picture. I don't have to see it to know what it looks like: a girl with straight brown hair and pale skin, standing beside her shiny new car, ready to begin the next chapter in her life. But he holds his camera out in front of him to show me the photo. I'm surprised by what I see; maybe Fiona wasn't just being nice the other day when she said I looked good. In fact, maybe I've never looked quite so good as I do right now, with my car and my surfboard behind me. Even in the photo, I can see that my eyes have some light behind them, just like my brothers' always did.

There is empty space on either side of me, space that my brothers would have taken up if they were here today. Maybe there will always be empty space on either side of me, the places where my brothers should be standing. And I know now that I will live with that empty space every day for the rest of my life.

"Oh," my father says, slipping his hand into the pocket of his jeans. "I almost forgot. This came for you in the mail."

He holds out an envelope addressed to me. No return address, not even a postmark, as though someone slipped it in our mailbox overnight while we were sleeping.

"Thanks," I say, taking it from him and ripping it open. I stifle a gasp when I see what's inside: a photograph with two handsome men—boys—tan and muscular, their arms draped lazily around each other, their surfboards propped up in the sand on either side of them. One of them has hazel eyes ringed in a yellow as bright as the sun, and the other's are icicle blue.

I hope my father doesn't see that my hands are shaking as I stuff the envelope and photo into my purse. I shrug like it's nothing, but my heart is pounding so hard that I'm surprised my father can't hear it.

My mother comes out of the house carrying a paper bag, Nana trotting along beside her. "Just some snacks for the road," she says, holding it out.

"You know there are, like, a million restaurants between here and Palo Alto?" I say, but I take the bag nonetheless. I lean down to kiss Nana goodbye and press my cheek to her soft fur.

"Drive safe," my mom says, hugging me tight. "And call us the minute you get there."

"I will," I say. "I promise." She offered to drive with me, but I turned her down. I want to make this trip alone, and now, as the picture makes my bag feel like it weighs a hundred pounds, I know why.

My father hugs me next, kissing the top of my head the way he did when I was a little kid. I wave to my parents through my open window as I pull away, the shadow of my surfboard visible on the driveway at their feet.

· · · · ·

At every red light between the glass house and the entrance to the freeway, I pull the photo from my bag and turn it over in my hands, gazing at it as though I think that if I just stare at it long enough, it will reveal all the answers. Maybe there's some secret message, some tiny writing stashed in the corner, hidden in the sea behind them.

But there is nothing. No hint, no clue. I don't even recognize the handwriting on the envelope. It could have been any of them—Jas, Pete, Belle, even Hughie or Matt—who sent this photograph to me.

Pete and Jas look so young in the photo, lanky teenagers; it must have been taken back when they were surfing together, before dust or Belle or I had a chance to come between them. Still, it's clear that Jas is the older of the two; he's taller than Pete, more filled out. Funny that I never knew exactly how old either of them was.

I pull onto the PCH and begin the drive up the coast. The next exit is one that I know well. One that no one ever takes. One that leads the way up above the water, where there are two ruined houses on opposite sides of the cliffs. The day I met him, Pete told me about waves that rose all the way up the cliffs, destroying some of the houses there. The storm that set off Witch Tree could have sent the waves that destroyed what was left of Kensington Beach, drenching Pete's house in salt water, pulling the stairs from the cliffs, and flooding the beach altogether. Maybe the ocean *did* swallow my memories whole, after all.

I could change direction right now, check the Surfline app on my phone and find out where the biggest swell is headed next, where on earth the best waves will be today, tomorrow, next week. I could turn around and speed to the airport, buy a ticket, check my board, and disappear. That was our plan, after all: to travel the world, chasing the waves together.

But I shake my head, resting the photograph on my lap. Pete always said that once you make a decision to take a wave, you shouldn't change your mind. No matter how big or how small the wave, once you paddle into it, the surest way to get yourself pummeled is to try to change direction instead of riding it out. I press down hard on the gas, speeding north, resuming my course.

The photograph is all I need right now. Proof that Kensington was real. Pete was real. Belle was real.

Jas was real. In my mind's eye, I can see him right now, on the other side of the world, taking wave after wave in an ocean as clear and cool as starlight. Long before he met me, Jas planned to chase the waves around the world—with Pete, not with me. He stayed in Kensington because he was waiting for Pete to go with him.

I remember it all, sharp and crystal clear.

I remember Pete: the way my hand fit in his grasp, how his skin was always warm, as though it was constantly basking in the sunshine. I remember his kisses and the way he tasted and the sprinkle of freckles across his nose that were just a shade darker than the freckles that dotted the rest of his body. I remember that he taught me to take a wave, stood up on the board behind me, and let me fly.

I remember Belle: her steely gray eyes, her blond hair flying behind her as she took a wave. I remember the gash in her leg, ugly and red, and I remember the way Pete held her as she bled. I remember how she looked at me when she told me the truth about my brothers; she was sorry, not just for having kept the truth from me, but also because she couldn't save them.

And I remember Jas: the smell of him, the feel of him, the taste of him, the weight of his body above mine, the strength of his arms around me. I've never met anyone so strong. He was strong enough to save me from the water; somehow, he got me onto the beach where they found me, even if all he did was push my body into the right current. And he was strong enough to save himself, to save Pete, to save Belle. Somehow or another, they made their way back onto dry land.

And somehow or another, someone wanted me to know it.

The photograph feels hot on my leg. I stuff it back into its envelope, press the envelope deep inside my bag, and steady my grip on the steering wheel. When I reach for it later, I'll discover a few fine grains of sand, sugar-white and flour-soft, resting at the bottom of my bag. For now, I'll keep heading north, just like I planned. For now, I'll live my life without knowing exactly where my friends might be. Because now I know that every minute we spent together was real. Our love was real, and someday I'll have the chance to say *I love you, too*. And that's enough.

But—maybe just one stop first. It's beach weather after all, just like my father said. I can practically feel the weight of the surfboard on the rack above my head. And it turns out I've already had a few lessons with an expert. I change lanes and head for the coast.

Just a few waves and then I'll resume my course.

For now.

ACKNOWLEDGMENTS

Thanks to the brilliant and endlessly kind Joelle Hobeika, Sara Shandler, and Josh Bank at Alloy Entertainment. Your unflagging enthusiasm and creativity never cease to amaze and inspire. Thanks also to Kristin Marang, Theo Guliadis, and Alloy's marketing team.

Thank you to everyone at Farrar Straus Giroux and Macmillan. Thanks to Wes Adams for razor-sharp editorial guidance. Thanks to Beth Clark for the beautiful cover; to Ksenia Winnicki, Katie Fee, Ellen Cormier, and the entire marketing and publicity team; to Angie Chen; and to *Second Star*'s copy editors, Kate Hurley and Karla Reganold, for their precision and patience.

Thank you, J. M. Barrie, for creating Wendy, Peter, Hook, and Neverland.

I became thoroughly obsessed with all things surf-related as I researched and wrote this book, and it all started with Susan Casey's riveting book *The Wave*, which I wholeheartedly recommend to anyone the least bit interested in surfing, waves, the ocean, or the planet. Thanks to every photographer and videographer who braved the elements so that landlubbers like me could Google video after video and watch superhuman surfers take big wave after big wave after even bigger wave.

Thanks to Sarah Burnes, Logan Garrison, and everyone at the Gernert Company. Thank you to my lovely writing group: Caroline Gertler, Caron Levis, Kristi Olson, Jackie Resnick, Julie Sternberg. Thanks to Mollie Glick and the team at Foundry. Special thanks to Anna Godbersen, and many thanks to Rachel Feld.

Thanks always to my parents, my sister, and the Gravitt family; and thank you to all the friends I've been lucky enough to meet along the way.

And once again, thank you for everything, JP Gravitt.

—A.B.S.

*Dogs are better than human beings because
they know but do not tell.*
—Emily Dickinson